HEAVENLY

Carol Bogolin

A KISMET® Romance

METEOR PUBLISHING CORPORATION
Bensalem, Pennsylvania

KISMET® is a registered trademark of Meteor Publishing Corporation

Copyright © 1993 Carol Ann Bogolin
Cover Art Copyright © 1993 Daniel O'Leary

First Printing April 1993.

ISBN: 1-56597-058-6

Printed in the United States of America.

To my sister, Mary, with thanks and love.

CAROL BOGOLIN

Carol Bogolin has always believed that if she thought she could do something, she'd try it. Whether it was knitting, recovering furniture, running a Religious Education program, directing choirs, raising three daughters, or teaching high school math and music, she gave it her all. Carol now lives on the beautiful Mississippi Gulf Coast with her husband and writes romance novels. Isn't life wonderful!

ONE

David St. John rushed out of the downtown Atlanta hotel's front door and frantically searched up and down Peachtree Street. Damn, where was she?

There, across the street. He sighed, relieved. She was heading into an all-night coffee shop with Phil, his old college friend. They were hard to miss. Phil was trying to squeeze through the door with two cases—one containing a violin, the other a cello. David grinned.

Knowing she was within reach, David took his time searching his tuxedo pockets. He pulled out his last allotted cigarette for the day and flicked his lighter. His hands shook, making the flame dance dangerously close to his cupped palms. He laughed exuberantly. The symptoms: shaky hands, sweaty palms. The cause: a new woman.

He inhaled the cigarette smoke, savoring the pungent kick of the nicotine and the heady delight of the chase about to begin. He took his time, enjoying both the cigarette and the anticipation. There was no denying that his body needed a woman's body—not when he was clamoring for release just from the glimpses he'd had of the lady this evening.

He crushed out his cigarette and sprinted across Peachtree, hopes of success mingling with fear that she might already belong to someone else.

He entered the coffee shop and, with the instincts of a homing pigeon, found her. Just like when he'd looked up at that evening's gala and had seen her playing the cello, his heart kicked into overtime, his stomach knotted, and his body temperature shot up. Never had his adrenaline flowed this fast!

He wove his way through the red Formica-topped tables toward her. *God, but she was gorgeous!* The closer he got to her, the faster his heart beat.

David looked at Phil. Tall, blond, and handsome. Was he dating the angel? No. No rings on either of their hands. She was fair game.

"Phil, you old son of a gun." David extended his hand to his friend—her companion.

"David!" Phil rose from the booth and, bypassing the handshake, hugged David. "How the heck are you? What're you doing in Atlanta?"

"I relocated my offices here some months ago. I saw you at the gala tonight and followed you here. Still like that long-hair stuff, huh?"

"Yeah. When you belong to a classical string quartet, liking that long-hair stuff is a prerequisite."

David turned to face the woman, nearly floored by the full, sensual lips formed into a shy smile, by the sleepy eyes that made her look thoroughly sated by a lover. Every man in the place must be spellbound by her.

"It was great seeing you again, Phil. We'll have to get together and rehash old times. Right now I know you must have to be running along, so introduce me to your companion and cut out, okay?"

She laughed. A sound so low and sexy, it shimmered

over his body and settled low in his belly. He slid into the booth next to her on the padded bench. Her perfume, wildflower-fragrant and subtle, aroused his already heightened senses. He inhaled deeply.

Phil began the introductions, "Kathlyn, my fellow musician." *Kathlyn. Unusual. Perfect,* David thought and introduced himself. "David St. John."

"As in, the gospel according to . . . ?" she asked.

She was quick. And breathtakingly beautiful. David felt his pulse quicken.

He turned toward her, resting one hand on the table-top, the other arm along the cracked red vinyl of the seat back. His hand lay close enough to reach out and touch the golden skin of her cheek. He resisted, knowing it was too soon.

"Are you already taken, angel?" She shook her head, and he felt like whooping out the Bulldog cheer. "I wonder why I haven't seen you before. You're a model. No. You're an actress, moonlighting as a cellist."

"You noticed me at the gala?"

How could I not have? Surely every man here had. But none of them was with her now, and David was going to increase his lead.

He lowered his voice to a more seductive level. "Of course I did. Hair like spun gold, a complexion like sun-kissed copper. Lips like that, and those eyes; how could I help it? You're Lauren Hutton's sister, aren't you?"

"Who?"

"Lauren Hutton, the movie star."

Her voice sounded husky. She sat, hand on chin, staring curiously at him. Her eyelids, which had rested at half-mast, had risen centimeter by centimeter with each of his compliments. Now the full, round circles of crystal-clear blue shone at him, and David was drawn deeply into their depths.

A caution flag went up. He momentarily slowed the chase. Through the fog in his brain he wondered about the feelings she invoked in him. Desire, surely. But something else unexpected. Something deeper, more tender—something almost lulling and peaceful. Odd. He had never felt like that before. Was this love at first sight? He could never allow himself to fall in love, but the concept of love at first sight might make an interesting clinical study. He'd have to remember these feelings for closer examination later on. Right now he had an urgent desire to bed this woman.

He put his elbow on the table, matching her posture. "You are truly lovely." Good Lord, how he meant that!

"Maybe we should get going, Kathlyn," Phil interjected, then yelled, "Ouch! What the hell was that kick for, Kathlyn?"

Kathlyn frowned at Phil and winced as he bent to rub his leg. She wasn't ready to leave. She looked up and watched David's puzzled look turn into a knowing grin.

Kathlyn groaned and buried her hot face in her hands. The man was an impossible flirt, a devil in disguise, but heavens, he was good at what he was doing. Her heart was going a little crazy, but deep down she knew he wasn't serious. Surely no one made advances this strongly with an old friend as a third-party witness.

She opened her eyes and peeked at him as he sat frowning at Phil. David's very dark brown hair curled rakishly around his head and down over the back of his neck. His scowl made his full black brows meet over the bridge of his nose, but his wicked black eyes twinkled mischievously. When he smiled, grooved parentheses formed to encase the heart-palpitating result. He turned his head away from her, and she wanted to touch the curls that lay against the collar of his formal white shirt, run her hands over the shoulders that filled out the black tuxedo. Devastating. That's what he was. And didn't he just know it!

"Oh, hell," he exclaimed impatiently. "A business acquaintance has spotted me. Excuse me for a minute, won't you?" He stood and gave Kathlyn a full-voltage smile. "Don't go away."

Phil sucked in his breath, ready to explode with a lecture. "Listen," he said. Kathlyn kicked him again, more softly.

"Damn it. Stop doing that."

"Sorry, but I want you to stay out of this. I'm dying to see what comes next."

"But, Kathlyn—"

"I know. He's way beyond my experience, but I've read and studied about the modern male and his different approaches to women. No one's *ever* tried anything quite like this with me. I'd like to see a real pro at work."

"You mean you weren't taken in by what he was saying?"

"Come on, Phil. Give me a little credit, won't you? I'm not long on experience, but I'm not exactly stupid, either. This is all rather thrilling."

Phil shook his head. "I swear he could make *The Guinness Book of Records* with his speedy approach. You don't suppose it ever works, do you?"

"You're asking me? Naive Kathlyn McDaniel?"

He laughed softly, then frowned. "I remember a time when David was shy and reticent. He's changed. I'll let you handle him . . . for now."

Kathlyn watched David shake hands with the man he

had been talking to and then weave his way through the crowded room of men and women. Some were dressed in formal attire, some in work uniforms, and some in plain jeans and T-shirts.

A distinguished silver-haired gentleman stopped David, and Kathlyn watched with fascination. He was shorter than she'd thought, perhaps five ten or eleven. He looked about thirty, but the way he carried himself and his savvy manner made him seem older. Kathlyn could almost feel his impatience to be rid of the man chatting with him. David kept his gaze on her, and she sensed his determination. Then he stalked toward her like a man on a mission, a man who would not be swayed from that mission. Her heart picked up speed and her hands began to sweat.

"Now, where were we?" He seated himself next to her again, this time closer. When he turned to face her, he brushed his arm against hers. He lifted his hand and trailed a fingertip down her cheek. It quivered beneath his touch. Spellbound, she saw his satisfied smile.

"So, what do you say, angel? Let's go make some sweet music together."

Stunned, Kathlyn jerked upright as if a puppeteer had yanked on her strings. Suddenly the onslaught to her emotions and his bold, brash approach tickled her funny bone. She put her hand to her mouth, trying to hold in the giggle. At the same time Phil jumped to his feet, yelling, "Now, see here, David!"

She laid a restraining hand on Phil's arm, and the giggle escaped. The one loose sound set off more. It wasn't long until she was laughing openly.

With one hand restraining Phil, she dabbed a paper napkin to her eyes with the other. "Sit down, Phil. We both know that Mr. St. John was only teasing."

"Like hell," Phil mumbled.

David looked at Kathlyn as if she were an alien.

"No, truly, Phil. If you weren't so buried in your music, you would know that really successful men don't use that pushy approach."

"Suppose a woman took him up on his offer?"

"Then I guess he'd have to decide if he wanted to share his body and himself with such a loose woman. Personally, I don't think he would. Mr. St. John seems more discriminating. . . . Pardon me?"

"I said," David replied, trying to keep the astonishment and laughter out of his voice, "my name is David." Were they reenacting some kind of fairy tale? "You wouldn't happen to have any dragons you'd like me to slay?"

"That was George."

"George?" David bristled at the sound of another man's name on her lips.

"Saint George slew dragons. David slew the giant."

"Oh." *What the hell, why not go with the flow?* "Well, any giants you want toppled?"

Kathlyn threw up her hands in a gesture of defeat. "Never mind. Shall we order something? I'm starved."

David stared at his menu. Somewhere in all that nonsense she had spouted, she had turned him down. Hadn't she? Yes, she definitely had. And he was glad! Oh, he'd win in the long run. Going slowly was going to be murder, but he liked a challenge. And this angel was going to be worth every bit of the extra effort.

She closed her menu. Her arm brushed his. Ripples chased each other all along his body. Here she was, the biggest turn-on he'd ever encountered, and he was glad she was not going to warm his bed that evening. This was nuts!

She chuckled, and the low, sexy sound stirred his manhood and then wrapped around him like a warm blanket. It made him want to rest in her arms, to let her keep his stressful dreams away. Damn, but he wanted that. He could never want her for a lifetime, but he'd take what little time he had. Damned if he wouldn't!

She chuckled again, and he snapped his gaze to her. "What?" His confusion made the word crisp.

"You're a terrible tease, aren't you?"

She grinned, and David found himself staring at her slightly uneven front teeth. He ran his tongue over his own teeth and imagined sliding it over hers. God, it hurt just to look at her. A tease? He couldn't believe she thought that. Either he was more exhausted than he realized, or his technique had gone to pot. Either way, he'd give it a rest for tonight. "Yes, I'm famous for my teasing."

"I'm sorry. I don't know where Phil's manners have gone. Let me introduce myself fully. Kathlyn Marie *McDaniel*."

David couldn't help himself. He just had to play with her. He gave her his best, practiced grin. "I would have guessed something more along the line of Diana, the moon goddess."

"Now, don't start again. I'm the product of a Scottish father and an Irish mother—two wonderful earthly people."

"Interesting." He studied her as if she were under a microscope, trying, and failing, to see beneath her beauty. Perhaps later, once he got used to looking at her. "I've always found the study of genealogy fascinating."

"You've always found the study of anything fascinating," Phil piped in.

David grinned. Phil grinned back, but his gaze darted to Kathlyn and then back to David in warning.

Kathlyn placed her order with the tired-looking waitress. "Hot apple pie à la mode, please, and a cup of coffee."

"Make that two."

"Might as well serve it all around," Phil added, snapping his menu shut.

While the men talked, Kathlyn sat back and wondered about David St. John. Why was he putting the make on her? He had just come from the benefit for handicapped children. There were lots of wealthy women there—beautiful women decked out in fashionable gowns and expensive jewelry. Why hadn't he picked one of them to take out, or to take home?

David shouted money. He dressed for success and oozed sex appeal. He was shouting, "Let me take you home to bed." He was not shouting, "Let me take you home to meet my mother." Kathlyn had a feeling that it would take a miracle for him to say that. She glanced heavenward questioningly, lips pursed.

"Naah," she murmured, lowered her gaze back to terra firma, and dug into her steaming apple pie.

"So how's your music going, Phil?" David asked between forkfuls of fruit-filled pie dripping with ice cream.

"So-so," Phil answered. "I should probably have gone into another field, but you know me—music's in my soul. I've finally reached my quota of students and landed a position with the symphony orchestra."

"Congratulations. I always knew your talent would win out."

He turned to Kathlyn. "Do you teach private lessons, too?" He had been trying not to look at her, but now, with his pie eaten and only his cup of coffee as a crutch, he had to. Twenty-five, twenty-six, he guessed, with a bone structure sculptors and painters would sell their souls for a chance to mold or capture on canvas.

She had full, nicely shaped breasts and carried herself proudly. He'd give anything to see her without the modest long-sleeved, white blouse and long black skirt. However, her gorgeous face held enough fascination for now.

He was so wrapped up in his feelings that he almost missed what she was saying. And that would have been a sin, for in the musical huskiness of her alto voice was a song worth hearing over and over. It soothed his ears, aroused his body.

"No, I don't teach privately. But between modeling assignments," she said wryly, "I teach choral music at Falcon High school. That's more than enough of a challenge."

"And you perform with the classical quartet." His mouth was working just fine without his brain—a good thing, since that organ was drowning in sensations that heightened with every word she said.

"Yes, I love the cello. Its melodious, enthralling."

Her voice was more melodic than any instrument he'd ever heard, and he'd be damned if he was going to let others be enthralled by it. *What the hell is wrong with you tonight? You've never had attacks of possessiveness.*

A fever suddenly shot through him—furiously hot, then chillingly cold. He'd never reacted to a woman strongly enough to cause flu symptoms. Later, during the day and when he was well rested, he'd see her again and find out if this whole reaction was part of a fever-induced illusion. He should get up and leave. But, being the genius that he was, he offered them both a ride home.

With a great deal of amusement, Kathlyn watched David tie her cello to the roof of his Alfa Romeo. The white interior of the car contrasted richly with the gleaming red exterior. The machine was well honed and mean. She had read those terms somewhere, and if this car didn't fit the description, she didn't know what would. She loved it—its ostentatiousness, its sink-in-and-relax interior. And she loved the way the man behind the wheel drove it with quiet confidence.

David dropped Phil off at his apartment, then headed across to the freeway and up to the northern section of Atlanta.

Kathlyn knew she should say something instead of sitting there absorbing the warming presence of the dynamic man beside her, instead of just inhaling the lime fragrance of his after-shave, staring at his hair-dusted hands, and recalling the feel of his finger skimming across her cheek.

The weather was a safe topic, but even she didn't dare resort to that. Finally she settled on music. Her taste was so eclectic that she conversed on rock groups and classical composers alike, trying to find out which he preferred. But David seemed more interested in learning than in adding his comments. If she'd quizzed him, could he have recited the information back word for word? She'd have bet a hundred dollars that he could.

At her apartment complex he untied her cello from the roof and came around to help her out of the car. She was already standing and waiting for him, hand outstretched for the cello case.

"I'll carry it." He began walking with her toward the gate, wondering why he had been surprised to see her standing alongside his car instead of waiting for him to open the door for her. She was a modern woman; they had only met this evening. It wasn't as if this were a date. But he couldn't shake the feeling that there was something old-fashioned about her. It didn't exactly make sense. She had laughed and taken his sexual come-ons rather well. Even though she'd assumed he'd been teasing, she hadn't blushed at what he'd said. She hadn't come across as a newly hatched chick, either. So why did he feel as if she was so different from other women?

He watched her insert a card into the security slot that opened the black iron courtyard gate. They walked in silence up the outside staircase to her second-floor apartment, where she unlocked her door and turned to take her cello from him. The moonlight played on her sensuous lips. The sound of the water bubbling in the fountain in the courtyard below simulated the flow of the hot blood pumping through his veins.

"I'd give anything in the world to kiss you, Kathlyn Marie McDaniel, but I think I'm coming down with the flu. It was a pleasure meeting you, angel." He touched his lips to her forehead, opened her door, and then handed her the cello. When she was inside, he reluctantly closed the door behind her, and silently vowed to see her again as soon as possible. The night air rippling across his heated skin chilled him as he rushed back to his car.

Kathlyn heard his retreating footsteps, and leaning against her door, she slowly slid down to the floor. She couldn't catch her breath, and her legs felt like French-cut green beans.

"Whew!" She expelled a gush of air. "That man should come with a warning label."

She looked across the dining area to the old, well-loved statue of the Blessed Virgin. "Well, Mary, what do you think? He has a great last name. You know that's always been my favorite gospel." Kathlyn sighed deeply. "I know. He's too much man for me, right? He's light-years ahead of me. I could buy out the bookstore on sex and love-relationship manuals, and he'd probably know more than the authors."

Kathlyn frowned and plucked at the carpet. "Just goes to show that I'd better get back to reading more of the one I did buy. The first couple of chapters didn't get me anywhere near to understanding men."

She picked herself up from the floor, stood her beloved instrument in the corner, then, with a whispered "Good night," patted the statue on the head.

She stopped at the entrance to the hallway leading to her bedroom and turned back to the statue. "You know what, Mary? Living alone here in Atlanta is difficult. In some ways life was easier in the convent."

TWO

"Guess you learn something new every day."

Kathlyn looked at her blurry image in the mirror and gave up on the fine points like mascara and eyeliner. She settled for a little blush and lipstick and then raced through the apartment picking up her schoolwork. "Lesson number twenty-seven. Do not read sex manuals right before going to sleep."

Her purse and car keys were in the bedroom. The sight of her unmade bed, rumpled from her twisting and turning the night before, had her recalling the long night of erotic images. Quickly leaving that room, she went over to pat the head of the statue. "God sure did make those particular feelings powerful, didn't He, Mary?"

On the short drive to school, Kathlyn could think of nothing but David. Of course, he would never take up with an innocent like her, but he was the stuff women wove into romantic tales. Tales or no, there was no way she could ever hope to marry someone like him. She knew her speed—Lyonel, the history teacher at school. When it came to women, he was shy and moved slowly. Kathlyn felt ashamed because she wished he'd speed up a little. She'd been seeing him for a month. All they'd done so far was to hold hands and kiss—just quick pecks good night. *Night. Bed. David.* The flash images made her tremble. He couldn't have been serious about sleeping with her. Why, he probably gobbled up green women like her for snacks.

She dragged herself out of her three-year-old Chevy and looked at the two-story Georgia brick school building. She groaned at what awaited her inside. Today was only Wednesday, hump day, but most of the students were already planning their weekends.

"You're using your talents. The job pays the rent. You're good with the kids.

A group of six sophomore girls rushed up to her, giggling, shouting, and fighting for her attention. Kathlyn lifted her gaze heavenward. *You had to make me this good?*

At the end of the school day, Kathlyn was more exhausted than the kids. *Only two more weeks until the spring concert!* Next week she'd spend four classes a day practicing in the auditorium. After school she'd be working with some of the students on choreography. The week after that she'd spend after-school and evening hours with the chorus and the jazz band.

Along with the four choral classes, she still had her two music appreciation courses to teach—general muck, the students called them.

As she walked out the front door of the school, Kathlyn took a deep breath of the warm springtime air and gazed at the glorious bushes of pink azaleas now in full bloom. She longed to take off her shoes and stockings and sink her bare toes into the carpet of green grass. *A tall glass of tea would hit the spot*, she thought.

She was so involved in the image of that tall, refreshing drink that she failed to notice the dark figure leaning against her car. When she did, the ice in her imaginary tea glass began to melt, and she flushed with heat, remembering last night's dreams. With great effort, Kathlyn got herself under control and walked toward the smiling man.

David leaned against the car in a nonchalant pose. The minute he'd seen her leaving the building, the pose had become a sham. Every nerve ending in his body was now on full alert. Daylight, good health, and rest hadn't changed his reaction to her one bit. When she took a deep breath of the spring air, her breasts lifted beneath her yellow-flowered blouse. The breeze played with the hem of her yellow, pleated skirt, caressing her magnificent honey-toned legs. His fever flared again. Her eyes widened when she saw him. He'd surprised her. *Good!* Since she had him so off balance, maybe he could even things up by doing the same to her.

"Hi." She sounded surprisingly collected.

"Hi, yourself."

He flashed his devil's grin at her. She hesitated, then, firm-kneed, kept walking toward him. "What brings you here? I haven't noticed any giants around."

"Neither have I." His chuckle nearly stopped her heart. "I came to see if you'd like to go to the soda shop."

Kathlyn laughed. "No, thank you. My students hang out there. I'd rather not have to explain you to them."

One of his sexy black eyebrows shot up, and so did Kathlyn's pulse rate. "Do they think their beautiful teacher doesn't date?"

"No, but I don't think they're ready to see me with someone like you." When he merely raised his brow again, she blurted out, "You know, such a good-looking man of the world." She was going to die of embarrassment!

"Thanks," he said humbly, but something in his tone made Kathlyn think he was beating his chest and giving the old Tarzan yell. He escorted her around to the driver's side of the car. "Okay, then we'll do something more adult."

Kathlyn hung on to the door of her now unlocked car and felt her blood rushing to her middle. "More adult?" she asked faintly, watching him walk around to the passenger side.

"Yeah, like go for a drink. How does that sound?"

Compared to what she'd been thinking, it sounded fine. "I'd like that."

She got into the car and started the engine. After he settled in, she took a deep breath and again inhaled the scent of his mouth-watering lime after-shave. As she reached for the gearshift between the seats, she brushed her fingers along his thigh. *Oh no!* She put the car in motion . . . carefully. "Where's your car?" she asked, trying to sound calm.

"I had my driver drop me off."

"You have a driver for your sports car?"

"No, for my limousine."

"I'll bet the kids got a charge out of seeing that in the parking lot."

"Yeah, well, it did cause a minor hurrah."

"No doubt. So you're rich, huh?"

"You could say that."

Kathlyn looked at him for a minute and then turned back to the road. "I'm not."

"What? You mean you aren't an eccentric with pots of money who teaches because she's called to it?"

Kathlyn relaxed at his teasing. "No, but I was called to teaching, and I'm good at it. I'm probably even eccentric, though I doubt it. I'm just ordinary, doing an ordinary job, trying to make a living at it.''

"But you'd like to be rich?" A warning signal fired in his brain, and David stiffened. Was being rich one of her goals in life? If so, how far would she go to achieve it?

"Not particularly." She shrugged her shoulders. "Knowing me, if I had money, I'd probably give it all away. So, what do you do, or don't you work?"

David was immensely relieved. Not that he would have minded spending a considerable fortune on her. *Just to get her into his bed*, he reminded himself.

"I accumulate companies," he said, thinking of the last three grueling days of meetings.

She flashed him a wary look. "How many have you accumulated?"

"Around fifty, I suppose."

Kathlyn choked. "Fifty? Holy cow! What do you do with so many? How do you keep up?"

"I don't actually run them, though I used to when there weren't so many. Now they're part of the conglomerate. Other people run them and send me reports. Miles and miles of reports." He leaned his head against the headrest and sighed tiredly.

"So you sit around all day reading reports? Sounds boring." David heard the disappointment in her voice.

"Some days it is, but some days it's very stimulating. Imagine trying to keep up with fifty companies. Trying to fix what goes wrong with them. Figuring out where they can make a better profit. The challenge is incredible." *Why am I trying to justify what I do?*

"And you love the challenge." Her tone was no longer disapproving, but admiring.

"My name is David. I can topple giants, remember?"

Kathlyn grinned and nodded her head.

"Speaking of challenges," he continued, "when are you going to go to bed with me?"

"When we're married."

David hid his grin. "Okay, then. Turn the car around and head for the courthouse. We'll apply for a license and get the blood tests. We can be married in three days."

"You got it, mister." She turned right at the next corner.

David started laughing about one second before Kathlyn did. She made another turn and pulled into her apartment's parking lot. "There's a marvelous pub right across the street. Let's go celebrate, shall we?"

When he met her at the rear of her car, David was still laughing. "You're a pistol, Kathlyn Marie McDaniel. I like your style."

"Yours ain't so bad, either."

He laughed again, enjoying the freedom of it. He used to laugh a lot. Still did, he supposed. But this felt different. More . . . free. He took her hand, savoring the shock waves racing up his arm, and led her across the street.

Kathlyn's arm was humming like a live wire. Interesting. She was proud to be with this distinguished-looking man in his blue power suit. He hadn't balked or run at the dreaded *M* word. Perhaps she should write to the editors of *Cosmo* and tell them that a way to find out if a man was afraid of commitment was to bring up marriage teasingly.

They entered the pub and found a small table near the back. Just as David was assisting her into a chair, she spotted Lyonel at a table in the corner. She almost called out a greeting, but noticed just in time that he and his male companion were holding hands.

Stunned, she quickly changed seats so her back was to the men. "Let me sit on this side."

David shrugged and motioned toward Lyonel. "Does that bother you?"

She looked down to her toes. "I've been dating one of them."

David had a sympathetic comment ready, but realized it might embarrass her if he said it. Again, despite the snappy conversation in the car, he had a feeling of trying to protect an innocent. This woman was beginning to puzzle him more and more. And he was finding this puzzle irresistible.

They ordered iced mugs of beer, and David's tense muscles began to loosen. Actually, he had started relaxing the minute he had seen Kathlyn at school.

"Ah, that feels good." She sighed.

David looked under the table and saw her yellow pumps lying next to her feet. "Rough day?"

"Let's just say, two hundred and forty rambunctious teenagers is more than enough."

"Surely the schools aren't that crowded?"

"No. The class limit for regular subjects is twenty. For music classes, it's forty. And believe me, that limit could be surpassed if everyone who wanted an easy credit was allowed to take them. I persuaded the principal to permit tryouts for chorus. Before this year, the class was first-come, first-serve. That made for an interesting, chaotic chorus. Most of the students last year couldn't carry a tune in a bucket, and then about a quarter of them didn't even show up for the concert. Now, you tell me, what's a chorus without a concert?"

"A lot less work?"

Kathlyn laughed. "No. It involves more work trying to keep those easy-credit students in line. This year most of my students enjoy singing. The concerts and performances are extra work, but the confidence they instill in the kids is worth the sacrifice.''

"You enjoy it, don't you?" David knew the answer before he'd asked, and at the same time felt a jolt of surprise. When had he last enjoyed, really enjoyed, his job? That was ridiculous. He *did* enjoy the wheeling and dealing of high finance and big business.

"Yes. Most days I love it."

"So when do you find time to model?"

Kathlyn drew her thumbnail through the frost on the side of her mug. "David, I don't model. I thought you were joking about that last night."

"Why would I be joking? You have fantastic bone structure. Your figure is perfect."

Kathlyn's face turned a dusky rose color. David stared, amazed. *She has no idea how really beautiful she is*. Staring at her face, into her blue eyes, he felt himself hardening. He was caught in her spell, captivated by her beauty, and befuddled that she was unaware of her magnetism. His breathing grew shallow, and this time he admitted that the fever wasn't caused by the flu. He felt as if he were sinking into some kind of quagmire. Why, in all his encounters with women, hadn't he ever felt like this?

A puzzled look came into Kathlyn's eyes. What revealing expression did he have on his face? He carefully schooled his features and took a sip of the cool beer. It did nothing to cool his ardor. Nothing would, as long as he kept looking at her.

"William." As if waking from a dream, David acknowledged the man standing next to their table.

"I thought that was you, David. Harry and Sam are here with me. Would you and your companion like to join us?"

"Sorry," David said as sincerely as he could, "but we were just leaving."

"Some other time, then." William nodded at Kathlyn and then turned back to his companions.

"Hell! Now we'll have to leave."

Kathlyn grinned. "I gather you didn't want to join them."

"Brilliant deduction. I just spent the better part of three days haggling with those men over petty things. The last thing I want to do is rehash it all on my off hours. Drink up, and let's get out of here."

Kathlyn took a sip of her beer, and David guzzled the rest of his. Once again he took her hand as they maneuvered their way across the street. He held it even after they had reached the safety of the other side.

He didn't want to leave her. "Would you like to have dinner with me?"

"I'm sorry, David. Truly. But I have an appointment."

"Another man?" He couldn't prevent the sharpness in his tone.

Kathlyn frowned. "No, I teach CCD classes tonight."

"What's that, some kind of civil defense course?"

"No." She laughed. "Religion classes at church. Confraternity of Christian Doctrine."

"Oh." He supposed somebody had to teach them; he'd just never met anyone who did. He tried not to sound too disappointed. "Is it all right if I come in and call my driver?"

"Of course." What shape was her apartment in? After rushing around this morning, it could look like a disaster area.

They stopped to get her mail, and climbed the stairs in silence. She sighed in relief that the dining and living rooms were in order. The kitchen wasn't too bad. She pointed to the wall phone above the kitchen counter.

David completed the call and turned to Kathlyn. "He'll be here in a couple of minutes. Could I use your bathroom?"

She couldn't let him see her bedroom. She ran down the short hallway and shut the door. The sight of the mussed bed had her going hot all over again.

"It's all yours," she said, pointing him to the bathroom door. She kept her face hidden and walked to the dining table to look at her mail.

When David emerged from the bathroom, he looked to his right and scanned the living room. Directly in front of him was a large, off-white couch with blue flowers and a multitude of plump pillows in various colors. The urge to lie down on it and fall asleep was almost irresistible. There was also an old but sturdy rocking chair. The floor lamp and magazines stacked next to it indicated frequent use. The far wall had a gas fireplace, and off to its side was a small, circular room full of light from the oversize windows. He walked around the couch for a better look at the little room and found a desk cluttered with school papers, a shelf containing music and books, and a straight chair with a music stand placed in front of it.

He came back around the couch ready to tell Kathlyn that he liked her apartment, but stopped when he saw her. Her head was bent over the letter she was reading. The smile on her lips confirmed that the message was a happy, welcome one. But what had his mouth dropping open was her hand. It was gently smoothing over what looked like a three-foot-tall old-fashioned religious statue. He could see white plaster where there should have been blue paint. One of the fingers of the folded hands was chipped, and whoever it represented was standing on—yes, it definitely was—a snake. David shook his head and covered a surprised oath with a cough.

Kathlyn's head snapped up when she heard the sound. "What?"

He tilted his head toward the statue. "A church garage sale?"

She put her letter down on the scarred, round oak table. "No, a Catholic-school-going-out-of-business sale. Come on, I'll walk down with you. I left my schoolwork in the car."

They left the apartment and arrived at the parking lot at the same time a black limo drove up.

"Must be yours."

"Must be.' He turned to her. "Listen, I'd like to see you again."

"You would?"

David sighed in exasperation. What the hell? Didn't she feel anything toward him? When he was around her, he could barely keep a normal thought in his head. "Yes. I jotted down your number. Can I call you?"

"I suppose you can."

"May I call you?" He thought she'd been correcting his grammar. That's what schoolteachers did, didn't they?

Kathlyn laughed heartily, and David's pulse went crazy. "Yes, you can, and you may."

He leaned close to her and kissed her cheek lightly. Feeling it quiver, he kissed it again and then **whis**pered into her ear. "I like your bathroom decor."

As the limo drove away, Kathlyn raised her hand and touched her cheek. The spot was still warm from his kiss, the surrounding flesh still tingled from his breath. She shook her head at the wonder of it. He wanted to see her again. He liked her bathroom.

Bathroom? Oh, no!

She rushed up to her apartment. Sure enough. Washed-out panties, bras, and panty hose hung at risqué angles from the shower rod. She'd never be able to face him again. Never! She shrugged philosophically and started laughing. "David St. John. You are one bad, teasing dude."

Her stomach growled, and on her way to the kitchen she stopped and smoothed a loving hand over the statue. "Not bad-looking, is he, Mary?"

In the tiny kitchen, she put a cup of water into the microwave and stared at it as it revolved. Sometimes she felt as if she were merely going around in circles. Was she destined to go back to the life she had left two years ago? The convent had offered safety, security, and serenity. Since leaving, she had often felt lonely and confused, like a fish floundering to get back into a stream.

No. She'd make it! As hard as starting over had been, she had made the right decision in not taking her vows. She'd be a good wife and mother. She loved teaching, she loved her students, and she'd love her husband and their children with all her heart. Sometimes she thought she'd burst from trying to contain all the love she had.

So where was this lucky man? She'd been patient. Well, as patient as a restless soul could be. She was reading the how-to books. She'd tried the singles' bars, the church socials, and the closest she'd come to a relationship was one month with Lyonel. And he was gay!

David's talk about her being a near goddess was baloney. She knew that. He wanted her in his bed. He wasn't the first to want that. He was, though, certainly the most puzzling, gorgeous, and—worst of all—interesting man ever to want her physically. But if he got her in bed, that'd be the end of their relationship, and the end of her dreams. She didn't have money or prestige to offer, but she did have herself—body, mind, and emotions. And all that, she'd give to the one man she'd love forever.

David didn't call that night, or the next, or the next week. Kathlyn accepted it.

According to the paper, David's business was thriving, had doubled its assets in the past two years. Even the analysts couldn't figure out how he could consistently take companies on the verge of bankruptcy and turn them into successful ventures. David was one of four people nominated for Atlanta's Businessman of the Year.

He probably thought she wouldn't fit in with his lifestyle. She would have, had she been the model or movie star he had thought she was. Not that she wanted to be either of those. She liked who she was, and so would her future husband. She had spent twenty-six years working on becoming the person she was now. She wasn't quite finished with the project—would probably only be when she died—but she hadn't turned out too bad so far.

Still, she wouldn't mind if David wanted to see her again. She liked the sexual tingles she felt when she was near him. She liked the excitement he stirred in her just by his presence. But he hadn't called. He wasn't the one. She'd been through this before. Why, this time, did she feel so hollow inside?

At ten-thirty the next Saturday night, David showed up instead. *Of course he'd pick Saturday night,* Kathlyn thought resignedly as she let him into her apartment. Any other night she'd still be dressed and in makeup from her teaching day. Tonight she wore a facial mask.

"Won't you sit down? I'll go wash my face and be right back."

David admired her composure. What other woman could act the gracious hostess with dried green stuff all over her face? What other woman's lips looked twice as kissable surrounded by green face cream? He really had it bad, wanting to kiss her despite all that goop. He sat down on her couch and felt his muscles uncoiling for the first time in over a week.

When she came back into the room, he nearly groaned. Squeaky-clean face and long, just-brushed blond hair. He wanted to pull her down with him on the couch, to kiss her and hold her and to fall asleep with her in his arms. And if he could just find the energy, he'd do it.

"Would you like something to drink?"

"Nothing, thank you." He tried unsuccessfully to hide his yawn. "Sorry. I've been working my tail off the last two weeks. I didn't want to go home because the phone just keeps ringing with latest developments in the negotiations for a company I thought I wanted to buy."

"You don't want it anymore?" She seated herself in the rocking chair across from him.

"To tell you the truth, I don't know. I'm just so tired. Can I . . . er, may I stay here tonight?" Her sleepy eyelids stretched open. She had the sexiest damn eyelids he'd ever seen.

"David, I . . ."

"Please? I don't want to go home. My answering machine can take the messages, and I can listen to them in the morning after I've had a good night's rest. I haven't slept in two days, Kathlyn."

Tempted to consider this another one of his moves, like the bold ones he'd used in the coffee shop, Kathlyn took a long look at his face. He did look exhausted. He had a day's growth of beard, and his deep, dark eyes were bloodshot. He was telling the truth.

"I guess it'd be all right." She got up to get him some bedding. "You know where the bathroom is. I'll make up the couch for you."

"Thanks, but I didn't mean to rush you off to bed."

She stopped in the hallway on her way to the linen closet. "I was going to practice my cello for a little while. I semi-soundproofed the bedroom, so it shouldn't disturb you." He walked closer and closer to her. She began to lose her concentration. "Uh, we have a performance at the Art Center tomorrow afternoon."

He stopped directly in front of her. Her pulse quickened. He smiled and ran a finger along her neck, and his brown eyes darkened to black.

"I want very much to kiss you, Kathlyn Marie Mc-Daniel, but as tired as I am, I don't think I'd be able to give you much pleasure. Especially if the kiss escalated to lovemaking. I'd probably explode with my own pleasure, then immediately fall asleep."

She ran her tongue over her parched lips. "I—I thought men couldn't . . . when they were exhausted."

"I guess that depends on the stimuli." David shrugged and then couldn't fight himself any longer. He had to have one little taste of her. Knowing it wouldn't be enough, knowing it would make him crave more, he lowered his head and placed his closed lips on hers. No tongues, or he would be lost. Even this— the softness, the willing pliancy of her lips, the electrical sparks starting at his lips, going down his spine, tightening his stomach muscles and below—was like dying and going to heaven. With what he was sure was superhuman strength, he raised his head and left her standing with eyes closed and lips pursed. He'd carry the enchanting look of her flushed, dusky rose face to his grave.

Kathlyn opened her eyes and slowly raised a shaky finger to her lips. "Oh, my," she whispered.

She went down the hall and brought out a set a sheets and a blanket and ducked into her bedroom for her extra pillow. She was making up the couch when his words finally penetrated her consciousness. He had sounded positive that they would automatically wind up making love if he really kissed her. Her heart was already shaking from the chaste caress they had shared. What would a real kiss do to her? Make her forget herself and go to bed with him? Didn't people have control over that? Surely there had to be conscious thought and a great deal more than a nodding acquaintance with a person before lovemaking?

He'd been talking about that since he'd met her. Maybe his come-on in the restaurant hadn't been a joke. She was beginning to think he had been totally serious. He'd assumed that if he hadn't had the flu that first night, he'd have come into her apartment. And he had talked tonight as if going to bed with her was an accepted fact. She felt like crying.

She wished there was more to what was going on between them than sexual attraction. However, if that's all it was on his part, she'd better let him know that going to bed with her was not an option. If he decided not to see her again, it was better now than later. Better, before what she was beginning to feel for him settled any deeper.

Just as she finished putting a clean case on the pillow, he walked out of the bathroom. He had taken off his tie and was unbuttoning his shirt. Dark curls of chest hair were revealed a little at a time. Kathlyn found them fascinating. Too fascinating. She *had* to get out of here.

Hurrying to the kitchen, she switched off the light. "If you get hungry or thirsty, help yourself to whatever you can find." She slipped the dead bolt home on the door and walked over to the statue. She looked at David and ran her hand unsteadily over the smooth plaster surface. "Good night," she whispered.

David watched her leave the room, her blue chenille robe hugging her backside lovingly. He wished he had the energy to hug her himself. He couldn't remember ever being this exhausted. Maybe he had had a mild case of the flu after all, and was feeling the aftereffects.

Stepping out of his slacks, he stopped and stared at the statue. Funny, but he'd had the distinct impression that Kathlyn had been saying good night to the statue more than to him. He shook his head at his whimsy and finished undressing.

Leaving on only his black briefs, he crawled under the sheet and blanket and squirmed around for a minute finding a comfortable position. Then he closed his eyes. Just as he did, faint strains of music wafted to him from Kathlyn's bedroom. The cello's sounds were as melodious as she had described them. He smiled and relaxed further. The refrain of an old sixties number drifted toward him, and he fell asleep mentally singing "The Twelfth of Never." That was a long, long time for love to last. An impossibly long time.

Kathlyn awakened to the soft buzzing of her alarm. It was her turn to lead the singing at eight-o'clock Mass. She had finally slept, after worrying about how to tell that gorgeous hunk of a man in her living room that she would not go to bed with him. She wasn't sure how to phrase it, but then, there was probably only one way—just do it!

She rose and dressed, gathered up her hymnal, and left her room. He was still asleep, zonked out like the exhausted man he was. Lying on his side, he had the blanket bunched under his muscular arm. She stared at his handsome face, at his curly hair, and remembered the heady thrill of his lips on hers. And she wished.

She shook her head to clear it of impossible dreams and quietly let herself out of the apartment.

When she returned a little over an hour later, David was gone. He had left a note thanking her for the use of the couch and saying he'd call. Kathlyn almost wished he wouldn't. There really was no sense in getting involved with someone like him. There was a man for her out there—a man who wanted a lasting relationship, not just a night in the sack. She wasn't the only woman in the world who wanted to go to her marriage bed a virgin.

There were so many other ways to show affection, to deepen the bonds between a man and a woman. Maybe David didn't know how to show affection. Maybe he thought sex was the way to show it. And maybe she'd take wings and fly!

She made herself some breakfast and practiced a little before getting ready for the afternoon's performance. And all the while she thought of David.

Before walking out the door, she raised her gaze to heaven. The trouble was, she didn't know whether to pray that David *would* call or pray that he *wouldn't.*

THREE

David entered the private elevator to his penthouse whistling "The Twelfth of Never" and thinking about Kathlyn, which was all he did between meetings lately. He liked the feeling of expectancy he got when he met a new woman. Possibilities like all the colors of the rainbow accompanied it.

The doors of the elevator opened into a magnificent white-tiled entryway where white marble statues of Greek gods stood sentry in the oval foyer. He walked onto the gray carpet of the living room and frowned. Why couldn't he have a normal life with a woman—a wife, children? What fates had decreed that he either have his soaring intelligence or a normal home life? How many times had he been willing to give up the first for the second? But no matter how lonely he was, the exchange was impossible.

So he'd have what he could. Kathlyn was a new conquest, a new source of delight. Hopefully their relationship would last long enough so he could experience as much of the rainbow's promise as he was allowed.

He raised his arms over his head and stretched his

muscles. When had he last slept so well? Maybe he should hire Kathlyn to play the cello for him every night. Maybe he should have her come play *with* him. An exciting prospect. After their kiss the previous night, she hadn't discouraged him. When he'd mentioned going to bed with her, she hadn't said anything. And that quip in the car about getting married was very well done. She was as sharp as a tack, and willing to give as good as she got. She was a woman who followed his thoughts and didn't shy away from his off-the-cuff comments.

But there it was again, that feeling that she was not what she seemed to be—more innocent than she let on. He remembered her hand resting on the statue as she said good night. He shrugged. He was not going to succumb to his habit of always searching beneath the surface. This time he was going to accept things at face value. If his mind would take a rest, he'd enjoy his relationship with Kathlyn Marie McDaniel, and perhaps his life would start to be more carefree.

Walking toward the phone, he stopped and threw his suit coat on the ivory-colored couch. He stepped out of his shoes and flung his tie toward a matching overstuffed chair. He punched the button on his answering machine and listened to the beeps and voices with only half an ear. He whistled that nostalgic song again and padded to the kitchen for something to eat.

He stopped in front of a gleaming white snack bar and stared with unseeing eyes at the black refrigerator. He wished Kathlyn had been there when he'd awakened. He wanted to see her in the morning with her sleepy eyes and shiny face, with her glorious hair mussed from her pillow, her skin warm and sleep-softened. God, he'd give anything to see her like that. Well, he *would*. It was only a matter of time.

He took bacon and eggs out of the refrigerator. How long should he wait before he saw her again? He knew he shouldn't appear overanxious. In the past, he had *not* been this anxious. If he showed himself to be too enraptured, women went all possessive on him. He'd learned to be casual when calling them and to never, ever, demand seeing them more than once or twice every few weeks. No way was he going to risk being taken for granted or, worse, trapped into a relationship he didn't want. So he'd call Kathlyn in a few days. He'd give her time to think about him, to wonder if he *would* call.

On Tuesday evening he called at six, seven, and eight. There was no answer. Remembering that she taught the CD thing on Wednesday evenings, he tried to get her right after school. Again, no answer. On Thursday evening, with bullheaded determination, he punched in her number every fifteen minutes. He gave up at ten o'clock. On Friday he accompanied movie star Doreen Langston to the premier of her new movie. When reporters took their picture, he smiled in smug satisfaction. *See, Ms. McDaniel, I'm not pining away for you!* After seeing the picture in Sunday's *Atlanta Journal*, she'd really be surprised to hear from him.

On Sunday he tried calling her at one o'clock. With great willpower, he waited until three to try again. On the eighth ring she answered.

"Kathlyn!" His voice exploded with relief and more than a little anger.

"Yes?" she puffed into the phone.

"Where the hell have you been?"

"Who is this, please?"

David swore under his breath, then counted to five and answered as calmly as he could. "It's me, David St. John."

"David!" she exclaimed excitedly. "Sorry. Wait a minute and let me catch my breath."

David grinned. All the waiting had paid off. She was breathless and thrilled to hear from him.

"Sorry about that, David. I was out doing my laundry. When I heard the phone ringing, I rushed up the stairs. I saw your picture in the paper with Doreen Langston."

His grin was so big, his cheeks hurt.

"What's she like? How did you get to go with her? Is she as funny as they say? Come on, David, tell all."

David's mouth dropped open, and then he had to close it to grit his teeth. He counted to seven this time. "I went to high school with her. Aren't you glad to hear from me?"

He shouldn't have said that. He shouldn't even have hinted that she was more than a passing fancy. He shouldn't show that he cared what she thought of him. And what did she think of him? He'd been so busy trying to get her aroused sexually and interested in going to bed with him, he hadn't even wondered about that. He had assumed she considered him sexy. Hell, he was more than passing in the looks department. But what else did she think about him? Hell. She was a puzzle like he'd never tried to solve.

"Of course I'm delighted to hear from you. I could hardly wait for you to call and let me know what Doreen is really like."

David rolled his eyes and gave up. Almost. "If you put on the coffeepot, I'll come over and fill you in."

"You're on! See you in a little while."

The phone went dead.

David took the receiver away from his ear and looked at it stupidly. "I'm still in control of this situation. I am!"

By the time he got to her apartment, he was edgy. *What kind of game is she playing? Is she playing one?* She opened the door. She was so lovely. Her blue eyes sparkled. Her smile was soft, shy. God, he was happy to be here.

He looked her over and grinned. She had dressed up for him in a kelly green, silky blouse and matching flared skirt. And . . . bare feet! Good God, her toes were naked—exposed to the sensuous texture of the carpet! Her toenails were unpolished, and a sudden replay of the scene from the movie *Bull Durham* flashed through his mind. He wanted to paint those nails and watch her squirm. He broke out in a sweat. Over toenails?

Kathlyn's heartbeat was going a mile a minute. David in a suit was breathtaking. In tight, faded jeans and a blue polo shirt, he was heart-stopping. She fought the urge to push back the two unruly curls that fell onto his forehead, and tried not to melt under the hot lights in his brown eyes. "Come in, please."

"I like your outfit."

Kathlyn wondered why he sounded so smug, but led the way into the living room.

"Thanks. I have a date later, and didn't want to cut our talk about Doreen short in order to get ready."

He squinted at her to see if she was teasing him. Was this a game of the *"You didn't call, so I'll show you I can get other dates"* variety? He studied her some more, but from the look on her face, he could tell she didn't even know how to tease like that.

Kathlyn seated herself on the couch, and David sat down next to her. She scooted a little away from him, turned sideways, and rested one leg on the couch under her skirt. She propped her arm on the back of the couch and looked directly at him. "So, tell me, David."

"Tell you what?" He liked the way the green material of her blouse stretched across her breasts.

She laughed, the blouse bounced, and David went under for the third time.

"About Miss Langston. How did you meet her? Why did she ask you to the premier? What's she like?"

"Okay, okay." He forced his gaze away from her breasts and gave in to her curiosity. "I met her in high school. We went to the senior prom together. After that we kept—"

"What was the prom like? Was she as beautiful as she is now? Were you the senior hunk that every girl was dying to go with?"

"What difference does all that make?"

"Well, you're the one who said you'd tell me about her. A few details would be nice."

David took a deep breath and then slowly let it out. "All right. A few details. I was a senior, and she was a freshman." *We were both the same age.* "I was no hunk." *Quite the opposite. In fact, I was your average, glasses-wearing, skinny genius.* "But I wanted to go to the prom. Doreen was beautiful even with her braces. I asked her." *After a lot of sweating and the breakout of a severe case of acne. And three months ahead of time so I could beat out the competition.* "She accepted." *Because her father made her go with the first guy who asked her, or not at all.* "She was gorgeous. She wore an off-the-shoulder chiffon creation in blue." *She was a goddess. My glasses had steamed up when I first saw her, and I nearly swallowed my tongue. I was only fifteen, so my father took us. She pouted all the way to the gym. Once we arrived, she laid into me and made me promise that she could dance with other boys. She stuck her nose in the air and entered the gym ahead of me. By that time, I wished I had never wanted to go to the stupid prom. It would simply have been one more normal experience I wouldn't have known.*

"David?" Kathlyn's voice interrupted his reverie.

"Oh, sorry. Anyway, we had a lousy time, and—"

"You had a lousy time? What did she do to you?"

His heart did a little flip. "How do you know that I didn't do something to her?"

"I just do. I'm right, aren't I?"

"Yeah. But, you have to understand that she was only fifteen. A freshman. Unless a junior or a senior asked her, she couldn't have gone. She was immature and rather puffed up since two of us had asked her."

"You and who else?" Kathlyn's eyes narrowed, and David got the impression that she was ready to do battle for him. It made him feel . . . great.

"The quarterback. You can imagine having to go with me instead of him."

"No, I can't imagine choosing anyone over you."

David sighed in exasperation. "Listen, Kathlyn, I was only fifteen myself."

"But you said you were a senior."

God, the woman was persistent. "I skipped a few grades. I was a nerd, a geek. I wore braces and glasses, and was shorter and skinnier than most of the boys in the freshman class." He had never told anyone that! How had she gotten it out of him?

"Personally, I think it was Doreen's loss, not getting to know and appreciate you. To a freshman girl, muscles, good looks, and eighteen are important."

"Actually, he was twenty. He'd failed two years in grade school." David paused. And then, for the first time ever, he laughed at that humiliating experience.

"Twenty?" Kathlyn chuckled. "He had to be desperate to want a fifteen-year-old."

"That's what actually brought Doreen and me closer

together. He had the hots for her. Foolish little thing let him talk her into going to the parking lot. I was out there brooding when he came on to her.''

"What did you do?"

"I hit him in a vulnerable spot." David smirked and Kathlyn blushed. "No, not there. I kicked his knee. Sent him to the ground, crying like a baby. Doreen and I have been friends ever since. She's nice. She's learned to look beneath the surface. You'd like her.''

"I guess."

David wanted to laugh at Kathlyn's antagonism toward Doreen. Then he saw the softness in her eyes, the compassion, and didn't know whether he cared for that or not. He changed the subject.

"What were you like in high school?"

"Oh, a Goody-Two-Shoes, I suppose. Always did my homework. Headed up all the committees. Listened to everyone's problems and obeyed all the rules."

Yes, he could see her—efficiently getting things done while others took the credit, always there with a shoulder to cry on, always willing to help.

"So you skipped a few grades, huh?"

He could tell by the tenacity of her questions that she was going to get it all out of him. "I'm a bloody genius." Even to his own ears he sounded egotistical.

"Hey. I'm impressed. I have so many questions, and then half the time I can't understand the answers. Like how a plane can defy gravity. What the black hole theory is all about.''

Absently she reached over and stuck one of her fingers in a lock of his hair. The tip of her other finger rested on his ear.

"So why," she asked, "does it bother you that you have an above-average IQ?"

David felt as if his hair had come alive. His ear

suddenly became his most erogenous zone. It took him a moment to register her words.

"Bother me?" he said sharply as he pulled away from her magic fingers. "It doesn't." *Except for those damn frustrating dreams. Except that my life can never be normal.*

She was seeing too deeply. What the hell was she, a witch? This was supposed to be a light romance. A temporary fling. Time to get things back on track.

He reached over and moved his fingers into the hair on the sides of her head. He leaned forward, purposefully. "You talk too much, do you know that?"

His lips descended and lightly touched the fullness of her lips. He raised up slightly. Then he lowered his head once again, teasing, lingering only for a second before releasing her, then back to play until her lips were soft and pliant under his, until they were searching for his whenever he broke contact.

"Oh, David." She sighed and lifted her hands to his head.

Now he had her!

The ringing of the doorbell sounded like a Chinese dinner gong. David jumped and tried to grab a mental toehold. Damn. He wanted to go on kissing her.

Her legs looked unsteady as she walked to the door. Her breathing was labored. She wanted him!

"Phil. Won't you come in? David's here, but he knows I have a date."

"David." Phil clasped his friend's hand while giving him a look of reprimand.

"Phil." David's reply was clipped.

David turned toward Kathlyn, pleased to see the tell-tale just-kissed look of her lips, her hair mussed from his fingers. His blood started rushing through his veins again. His manhood started hardening and would soon be an embarrassment. He quickly kissed her cheek. "I'll see you soon. Thanks for the coffee." Had they had any? He smelled the aroma of it in the air, so she must have offered him some.

He nodded to Phil and let himself out of the apartment. Once the door was closed behind him, he took a deep breath of fresh air. *God, that lady packs a punch.* He gulped in more air and felt steadier.

He walked away from her door. On the whole, the seduction of Kathlyn Marie McDaniel was progressing nicely. He could see the blinding light of sexual bliss at the end of the tunnel. He mentally patted himself on the back. She was getting closer to surrender. He was on course. He knew exactly where he was going and how to get there.

He reached the dead end of the outside walkway and retraced his steps to the stairwell.

"Let me get my shoes and purse, Phil, and I'll be ready to go."

"Take your time; I'm early. I'll help myself to a cup of coffee."

Kathlyn blushed and rushed down the hallway to her bedroom. She had forgotten to serve the coffee. Once she'd seen David standing outside her door, she'd forgotten everything except him.

"Where's Sandra?" Kathlyn frantically brushed through her tousled hair.

"We'll pick her and her brother up on the way to dinner."

Kathlyn quickly added gloss to her tingling lips and tried not to think about the teasing kisses that had been more potent than anything she'd ever experienced. "What's Sandra's brother like?"

"Mark? He's a great guy. Runs a chain of self-service laundries. You'll like him."

Kathlyn sincerely hoped so. Every blind date she'd had had fizzled out. Every time she met a new man, she wondered if he was the one. After meeting David, the man tonight would really have to be something special.

"What?" she called to Phil.

"I was just wondering how serious this is between you and St. John. I remember in college, his last two years, anyway, he had the entire freshman class of girls fighting to go out with him. I want you to be careful."

So David's awkwardness hadn't lasted too much longer than his high school years. She'd bet that Doreen Langston had fought just as hard as all those others to go out with him then.

"There's nothing serious between us. I'm not likely to hold his interest for long. Don't worry about me."

She walked into the dining room and joined Phil. "How are things going with you and Sandra?"

"Fine." He blushed, but his eyes lit up. "She accepted my proposal last night."

Kathlyn whooped with joy and threw herself into his arms. "Phil, I'm so happy for you both. You took long enough, but I knew you two would work things out. You belong together."

"Thanks, Kath. I love that woman. Imagine, she'd been willing to marry me when I didn't have enough money to support us. She's something, hey?"

"Yeah, she's something. Now, let's not keep her waiting while we stand around and chitchat. Are you sure you want her brother and me tagging along?"

"Yes, I'm sure, brat. Let's go."

Mark was delightful. They laughed a lot and enjoyed each other's company. Good thing, too, because Phil and Sandra were completely wrapped up in each other and plans for their wedding.

Mark saw Kathlyn home and stayed for a cup of coffee, one she actually made *and* served. They talked about music and plays and books and teenagers. He told her about his start in the laundry business, and how it had multiplied into a chain of ten stores. He was humble and uncomplicated, good-looking in a blond, blue-eyed sort of way, tall and well built. He was interested in everything about Kathlyn. Her equilibrium was completely in balance the entire evening.

So why was she longing for a little topsy-turvy thrill?

As far as Kathlyn could tell, David called on Monday night simply to talk. She mentioned her concert the following Friday evening and told him how busy she would be that week. He told her that he had to go out of town for a few days to straighten out a tangle at one of his businesses. He sounded excited to be going out into the field. Why had he opted for an office job?

"Sweet dreams, Kathlyn Marie," he said in closing.

"Sweet dreams to you, too, David."

Her night was indeed full of dreams—all involving a certain curly-haired, devilish, grinning man.

By Friday night her students were as ready as they were going to be. The curtain rose. The band played their opening number while the chorus processed onto the stage. Their singing was marvelous. Kathlyn was so proud, she could barely stand it. The patriotic numbers, the beautiful classical selections, all sounded to her biased ears as good as a performance by the Mormon Tabernacle Choir.

After the band selections, the senior chorus and band members combined their efforts in a tribute to the history of popular music. They started with old Tin Pan Alley tunes, marched through a little Sousa, Charlestoned through the twenties, jitterbugged into the forties, strolled, cha-chaed, and jitterbugged again through the fifties. They twisted to a Chubby Checker hit, protested via Bob Dylan, and danced to a present-day rock number. Everyone, including Kathlyn, was sweating, clapping, laughing, and rejoicing with the students.

The audience gave them rousing applause. The students gave her a dozen roses and a pendant in the form of a musical note, on a gold chain. She laughed and cried along with them. She sincerely hated to see some of her seniors leave, but rejoiced with them in the celebration of what they had accomplished and what was still ahead of them.

David left the auditorium still caught up in the enthusiasm. He felt as if his feet would not allow anything as simple as walking. He stood outside the doors watching the parents and students laugh and talk and congratulate Kathlyn. He couldn't remember being prouder of anyone.

As the throng filtered away, he walked to Kathlyn's car and waited for her.

He still couldn't believe he was there. He'd arrived home from Portland that afternoon and had gone to his office. The heady thrill of his on-site inspection had soon turned into a soaring headache in the confinement of his office, under the suffocation of paperwork. He'd suddenly needed, no, wanted, to be with Kathlyn. He'd squeezed into the auditorium seat prepared to endure the amateur concert. But he'd actually enjoyed it. In fact, his feet had tapped and his hands had clapped right along with everyone else. He could still feel the music zinging in him.

Kathlyn was elated. Too tired to move, too excited

to stand still. And then she saw him. He had come! Come to a simple high school chorus production when he could have been at a New York Broadway musical. She hiked her long black skirt up to her knees and ran straight into his arms. He lifted her and swung her around while they both laughed and kissed and laughed some more.

"You were great, Ms. McDaniel. Your students were great. Life is great!" He set her on her feet and cupped her face in his hands before smacking a hearty kiss on her lips.

"I'll follow you home, and then, if you want to, we'll go out and celebrate."

"You're on!" She quickly climbed into her car.

She grinned all the way home. She didn't know why he had come, and she wasn't going to ask.

"Hungry?"

"And thirsty." Her mouth felt as if it were lined with cotton.

He took her to one of the restaurants high atop a hotel in downtown Atlanta. The maître d' greeted David by name, gave them the best table available, and offered the wine list.

Kathlyn ordered a large glass of water; David, a bottle of the finest champagne. She gulped the water, and they toasted with the champagne.

"To your success tonight, Kathlyn."

"To the students."

David shook his head. "It takes leaders, Kathlyn. Those kids couldn't have done it without you."

"Nor me, without them."

David quit arguing.

They ordered light dinners, and Kathlyn glanced out of the restaurant's window. The lights of the city far below made Atlanta look like an enchanted land. She dismissed the scene and turned her attention to David— a Prince Charming in a charcoal gray business suit. "How was your trip?"

His eyes glowed with excitement. "It went well. That business is once again headed for success. Have you ever seen paper being made from wood?"

"Not recently," Kathlyn said wryly. "Come on, quit teasing and tell me."

David knew he was a little unusual, always wondering how things were made. And he knew that most people didn't care as long as they could use the finished product. But he was learning that Kathlyn was not like most people. Her eyes were sparkling with interest. Well, this wasn't the black hole theory, but . . .

"First, they have this machine, a drum, that takes the bark off the wood. Then it goes into a chipper." He explained the process. He even drew figures on the cocktail napkins. As he finished, it dawned on him that she might be bored to tears. Damn! He always got so involved.

"So, what do they do about recycling?"

"Huh?" He couldn't quite believe she'd asked a question instead of yawning.

"What about recycling? Did you see them do that, too?"

David smiled and told her how they cleaned the used paper and made it into pulp.

"You should teach. Your explanations are understandable and fascinating."

"I don't think I'd be any good. But thanks for the compliment."

He needs a challenge, Kathlyn thought. He's not satisfied with what he's learned or accomplished. He needs to seek other pieces of information constantly.

The food arrived and was delicious. the wine added to her mellowing. Conversation slowed, but just looking at David was more important than talking.

He asked her to dance. The music was soft and romantic, the lights dim and concealing. The minute she was in his arms, the world melted away. She sighed and rested her head on his broad shoulder, her forehead against his neck. His body heat was comforting, like a quilt on a chilly night. His after-shave transported her to the great outdoors. She felt safe in his arms and nestled closer.

David was going out of his mind with wanting her. And yet he loved just holding her against him. She felt so . . . right. He felt so . . . content. She smelled like a field of wildflowers, and he pictured them lying among the fragrant blooms, making love.

She yawned and her body leaned more heavily against his. "Tired?"

"Exhausted. I guess I've come down from the high of the concert."

He was going to take her home. Right now! He was going to escort her up to her bedroom and awaken another high in her that had nothing to do with music and everything to do with sex. Good sex. Mind-blowing sex.

She fell asleep on the drive home. Good. She'd need her rest, because he had no intention of leaving her side or her bed until Monday morning.

As he drove, he pictured it in his mind. She'd be nestled among the sheets, raising her arms, beckoning him to join her. Then he would be touching her golden body—his hands and tongue and teeth and lips and body feeling her, tasting her, rubbing against her and over her. He'd felt women before. He'd tasted them, too. But he knew—damn it, he absolutely knew—that with Kathlyn it would be so much more than with anyone else.

The culmination would be joining his hard, straining body with her soft, yielding one, and . . . and if he didn't stop thinking about it, trying to imagine feelings he knew would surpass his imagination, he was going to join his car with the unyielding interstate divider.

He wiped the perspiration from his forehead. He dried his hands on his suit pants. He turned the radio on to the soft listening station, praying it wouldn't awaken Kathlyn. The last thing he needed right now was to hear her low, sleepy voice.

The disc jockey was playing the hit song from the movie *Beaches*. Bette Midler was singing about someone being the wind beneath her wings. How could anyone allow himself to become so dependent on someone else? Let that person be the driving force in his life? Sure, everyone needed someone, sometime. But a person should only rely on himself. If he needed someone to hold him up, to carry him through life, then he was weak.

He parked in Kathlyn's lot and smiled as she gradually awoke. He still had trouble breathing when he looked at her, but he was coming to like what was on the inside, too. She was special. Talented. She relaxed his restless soul and made him long for the finer, gentler things in life. He liked being with her, and he saw no reason not to indulge himself as long as they didn't get serious.

He helped Kathlyn from the car, letting her rest against his side as they dreamily strolled up the stairs to her apartment. He helped her open the door and gently closed it behind them. He turned her and pulled her close. It was time to start building up the kiss that would send them both spiraling into sexual delight.

Like that day on the couch, he gave her teasing kisses. He brushed his tongue across her upper lip, then enticingly sucked on the lower one. She made the sound he longed to hear—the back-of-the-throat moan that indicated pleasure and arousal. The sound, in a pitch lower than her normally low register, sent waves of anticipation up and down his spine. The pressure against his fly was becoming obvious and powerful. He clamped his lips to hers and supped. She moaned again, and he had to draw back for air, for composure.

He dipped back for more, sipping, tugging, wanting her to open her mouth for him. He ran his tongue over her lips, hinting, enticing. The waiting became unbearable, yet more exciting by the second. He knew by her movement against his arousal that she wanted the joining, too. He teased her into opening her mouth.

"Come on, angel, open up."

"What?" she mumbled, lifting passionate, sleepy eyes to his.

"Come on, baby. You know what to do."

She shook her head.

"Open your mouth. Where have you been, in a convent?"

"Yes."

His head bounced back as if it were on a spring. "What?"

"I said, yes. I've been in a convent most of my life. Now, shush and teach me what to do."

"Like hell I will!" He winced at his language and tried to pull his sexually clouded thoughts together. Damn it all, a man shouldn't have to turn off his body so abruptly.

"Why won't you teach me?" Her voice was as rough as his felt. "Someone has to. And you're the best kisser I've met so far."

"Well, goody for me. I'll be damned if I'm going to kiss a nun." Much less do everything else he'd had on his mind since meeting her.

"Oh, for crying out loud!" She dropped her arms from around his waist and stepped back. "I'm not a nun. I prepared to be one, but found out it wasn't my calling. I left, and started over. You have something against that?"

"No, but, dammit, you should have told me sooner, not just sprung it on me like that." Yeah, she should have told him much sooner so that he could have gotten out before he'd begun to like being around her so much, before he'd begun to long for her comforting presence.

Kathlyn laughed bitterly. "When should I have told you? When you were dishing out the syrupy flattery? Or perhaps when you invited me to your bed? What difference does it make? I'm still who I was when you met me and kissed me."

"I don't know why it makes a difference, but it does." He was lying through his teeth. He knew why. Because sex had been his main objective. Still was, wasn't it? Damn, he hated being confused!

"I'm not stupid, David. It matters because I won't go to bed with you. Now, *that*, I should have told you a long time ago. I guess I kept hoping you'd change your mind."

"Hardly."

"Then I'm sorry for leading you on. I enjoyed being with you. Too much, I suppose."

She felt like crying. She also felt like screaming at him that there was a lot more to her than her body. She felt like slugging him, and, God help her, she felt like throwing herself into his arms and letting him take her.

She swallowed back her tears, trying to talk through

the huge lump in her throat. "Thank you for finding me attractive. It's quite a boost to the ego. I also thank you for tonight's dinner and—"

"Shut up, will you?" She looked so sad that he wanted to take her in his arms and protect her from guys like him. "Just shut up!" He yanked her back into his arms and gave her a rousing farewell kiss.

This time she opened her mouth and let him in. The shock of her inexperienced tongue had David going rigid. Helplessly he gave in to and shared the splendor of the kiss. Her taste alone was driving him to the brink. It was as sweet as honey, intoxicating as the finest Irish whiskey.

As primed as he was, he couldn't take too much of her heavenly mouth, and so he forced himself to halt.

"You sure don't kiss like a nun." His voice sounded like dry wind rustling over gravel.

"Thanks." She ran one finger over his upper lip. The look on her face was one of wonder. "You kiss like sin."

She laid her head against his chest and listened to the rapid thumping of his heart while trying to calm her own chaotic feelings.

David wrapped his arms around her and held her close. "I want you."

"I know," she replied, not looking at him, not daring to see the longing in his eyes.

He sighed deeply, having expected her to say she wanted him, too. "That kiss was erotic."

"Yes."

"Exciting."

"Oh, yes."

"And . . ."

She lifted her head and smiled at him. "New."

"Oh, Lord." David groaned and pulled her against

him once more. He rested his cheek on top of her head. He should have paid more attention to the puzzle solving. He'd have seen the innocent virgin in her, instead of deluding himself about her savvy.

He released her from his hold, feeling somehow lost and alone. "I like you, angel. An awful lot."

She smiled her heart-thumping smile. "I like you . . . an awful lot, too."

He shoved his hands into his pockets to keep from reaching for her again. "I'd better go."

Kathlyn nodded and then went to open the door for him. With one hand on the knob, she turned to him. "I'm sorry to have dumped that convent thing on you so bluntly."

David grinned, remembering the shock he'd felt. Then sobered, thinking about all he'd wanted to do to her. An ex-nun!

He felt his face heat up, ducked quickly to snatch a hard, swift kiss, and then let himself out of the apartment.

Kathlyn stood looking at the closed portal, wanting to call him back, wanting more of his kisses, wanting him.

Now that he knew she wouldn't go to bed with him, she'd probably never see him again. Tears filled her eyes. Sometimes life just wasn't fair. She'd had a glimpse of heaven on earth, and then . . . poof!

Trembling, she locked the door. She stumbled over to the statue and patted its head. "Better now than later, huh, Mary?"

But the remembrance of his kiss, his jaunty smile, the joy she had felt when she was near him, stayed with her all night—along with a guilty regret that she would never know the thrills to be found in his bed.

FOUR

"Hi Mom."

Receiving no reply to his soft greeting, David entered the nursing home room. The big, brown, comfy recliner in which he and his mother used to sit and play word games or read stories sat next to an oak end table. He smiled when his gaze encountered the imitation Tiffany lamp. His mother had brought the ugly thing home from a garage sale when David had been seven or so. She'd plunked it down and told him to fix it. He had. The neighborhood garage sales did a booming business after that.

He heard a sigh and turned toward the sound. He almost cried at the sight of his once beautiful mother now scrunched over the long table. Her hair was disheveled, as if she had not bothered to comb it for days. Its once glorious sable brown was now salt and pepper. Her loose robe hung limply from shoulders almost too weak to bear its weight.

"Mother," David called softly.

Sarah lifted her head and scowled at the intruder. He smiled into the scowl. Her dear face transformed with her welcoming smile. "David. Come see what I'm working on."

He came forward and dropped a kiss on the soft, crinkled cheek. "You look like hell, Mother."

Sarah laughed. "Who cares? Look here. I've been working on the mathematical problem we found in that textbook last week. Remember, the one that was supposed to be impossible to solve? Well, stand by, world. I believe I'm close."

David grinned and looked down at the legal tablet on the table in front of her. He glanced around and saw ten or more tablets all covered with figures. Could it be? Could she be getting back some of her abilities? David's heart was racing with hope. He picked up the tablet in front of her and scanned the pages.

Numbers. Mathematical symbols. The pages were filled from margin to margin. But not one of them followed any sequence or made any mathematical sense. His throat filled with a lump that was both pain and sorrow.

"You're the only one around here who could make any sense out of the problem. What do you think, David? Am I on the right track?"

Fifteen years. Fifteen years of watching his mother try to struggle within a world of genius gone defunct. Fifteen years of trying to figure out why the driving ambition to solve constantly had not been taken away at the same time her capabilities had.

Fifteen years of guilt, because if she had not had him, she could have left her husband, who grew more and more irritated with her dreamy stares and spells of mind wandering.

And fifteen years of anger at the woman sitting here for foolishly thinking that she could abandon her genius and settle down into a "normal" life-style as wife and mother.

That foolishness had cost her everything. Such a waste to the world, which would have benefited from her abilities. Such a waste to the man who had loved her without knowing of them. And such a waste to the son who loved her beyond all others.

"Come on, David. Quit daydreaming. Oh dear, I sound like your father. What do you think? Am I getting close to the solution?"

David looked down at the scribbling. He looked up at his mother, her eyes shining in hopeful expectation and pride. Perhaps the good Lord did know what he was doing. He may have taken away her abilities, but the hope and activity were keeping her going. But going where?

He cleared his throat. "Mother." He paused, prolonging the suspense. "I believe you have solved it."

"David!" Her voice rang with astonishment and laughter. And then the tears flowed. "Oh, David, I did it! I thought I could. I honestly thought I could.

"I have to get these in order and copied and then sent off to Professor Hilton at the university." She gave out a deep, tired sigh and leaned back in her chair. Her voice was a mere whisper. "I did it!"

David began stacking the yellow legal pads. "Mother, you did enough. I know your writing well enough to do that for you. I'll make sure Professor Hilton gets these."

"Thank you, son. What a dear, dear boy you are."

David busied himself with the tablets on the table. When he turned to her, he forced himself to smile. "Right now, though, I am going to brush your hair and see that you settle down for some much-needed rest."

"That sounds heavenly."

He helped her from the chair, trying not to notice how light she was, how many more pounds had been shed during this last intense work she had been doing. He tried not to notice because she was content and happy in her own little world.

He settled her on the bed sideways and sat behind her. He picked up her brush from the nightstand and began running it through her hair. She winced a little when he hit a snarl, and David gentled his strokes. He remembered doing this same thing many evenings.

Sarah's head was lolling from side to side when she spoke. "Your father came to see me yesterday."

David's hands stilled and his knuckles turned white on the brush. His eyes filled with tears. *Come on, Mother,* he begged silently, *you have to remember that Father's dead.*

Sarah's head turned toward him, and David gave up on his silent prayer. He started brushing again. "What . . . what did he say?"

Her tone of voice was dry and harsh. "He yelled at me, again, for not telling him about my abilities before we were married. And then he *said* he loved me."

"You don't believe him?"

"I imagine he did, in the beginning. You know what he was like later—constantly demeaning and angry."

David wanted to shout at her, to shake some sense into her. Instead, he kept his voice calm. "He didn't know why you were lost in thought so often, Mother. If he'd known, surely he would have supported you."

"I'm not so sure. I've told you. For people like us, there is no normal life. I'd seen too many failed marriages among my colleagues. I knew I could either have one life or the other. Your father and I should have had an affair, with no commitment on either side." Her voice softened and she turned and kissed David's cheek. "But then, I wouldn't have had you, would I?"

"Hi, Kathlyn."

"Hi, David."

Her voice sounded sleepy, but she knew who he was this time. "Did I wake you?"

"It doesn't matter. Is something wrong?"

Yes! My mother is sick. My whole life is going to hell, and I never should have been born! "No, I just felt like talking to you. How was your day?"

Kathlyn sensed that he needed a diversion. She gave it to him in the way of humorous incidents that had occurred at school. By the end of the telling, she could hear the relaxed, natural laughter in his voice. She wondered at the cause of his sadness, but didn't feel she had the right to ask again.

"Thanks, angel," he whispered.

"You're welcome, David," she whispered back.

David hung up the phone smiling and wondering what had inspired her to join the convent? Why would she give up all the pleasures of life? And after making that decision, what had it taken to uproot herself and begin again? Sure, he'd started new careers, but not ones that involved the magnitude of Kathlyn's changes.

He looked around his apartment and scowled at the decadent gods loitering in his foyer. He thought about the chipped, faded statue standing in Kathlyn's apartment.

He shed his clothes on the way to his bedroom and the shower. He stopped with one hand on the bathroom door and sobered immediately. Was he going to see her again?

No. Definitely not. He wasn't sure he could be with her and not desire her. The ex-nun radiated pure, unadulterated sex, but she wouldn't go to bed with him.

He was looking for an uncomplicated, no-strings-attached affair. Evidently almost-nuns didn't have those. In all likelihood she was looking for marriage, and marriage was definitely not in the cards for him. He'd be better off not calling or seeing her again.

He called her on Tuesday evening. There was a chamber of commerce banquet on Saturday night. As one of the nominees for Businessman of the Year, he needed to attend. In a big crowd he could surely keep his hands off Kathlyn. If only he'd stop picturing himself making love to her. However, he owed her something for lifting his spirits the other night. She'd get a big charge out of seeing movie stars and political figures. If she couldn't go, it was no big deal.

She hesitated. "I don't know, David."

He tempted. "Doreen's going to be there. Along with her costar, Jeremy Stanton."

"Why me? You could go with someone who's used to those things."

Who was he trying to kid? If she didn't go, it *would* be a big deal. He didn't want to go at all. He hated the effusive praise given out at these affairs. But since he had to go, he wanted to be with Kathlyn. She'd make it fun.

"Please," he begged, and wanted to kick himself for doing so.

"Okay, I'd love to." She laughed that sexy laugh right into his ear. Goose bumps made him shiver, wanting the one thing he couldn't have with her. He wished she'd said no. He was glad she hadn't.

"You'll need a fancy dress."

"I have something. What time?"

"I'll pick you up at seven."

"Thanks for asking, David. I'll see you then."

*   *   *

Kathlyn opened the door to David's knock. Her dress was black. Sequins sparkled from the round neckline, over her generous breasts, into the dip at her waist, and ended at the vee below. Three tiers of black satin ended above her knees, and from there on down, it was miles of sexy legs encased in sheer, black hose. Her black heels added to the already mouth-watering shape of her calves. On the short sleeves of the dress were little black beads. David wanted to flick them and run a finger over the golden skin of her arm. All he could say was, "Lovely."

"Thank you."

His gaze went to her face, and what little breath he had was knocked out of him. She'd made up her face with a light touch, just enough to enhance the natural color and bring out the sultry look in her sleepy blue eyes. Enough to highlight her high cheekbones. David wanted to smother her face with kisses, to taste again the sweetness of her lips and make them rosier than they were now with their light coating of pink lip gloss. Tonight might be the first test he had ever failed in his life. It was going to be hell keeping his libido in check.

He should have stuck to his decision not to see her again. His whole perspective on life changed when he was with her. With other women, the fact that he could not marry hadn't bothered him, except for that childish desire to have what he couldn't. In fact, he admitted shamefully, knowing he would not marry had worked to his advantage in his transient relationships. With Kathlyn he was beginning to imagine the whole ball of wax—a "normal" life. He'd better watch himself. "Shall we go?"

"If you'd rather not," Kathlyn whispered hesitantly.

"What?"

"You were scowling. I thought you had changed your mind about taking me."

"I'm sorry. I was thinking about the injustices of life. Are you ready?"

"Sure. Let me get my wrap."

She walked away from him, her carriage stately, her blond hair flowing over her shoulders. The least he could do was show her a good time on what was their last date. He steeled himself to enjoy the evening. When she rejoined him with a black shawl draped over her shoulders, he even managed what he hoped was a creditable smile.

"I suppose the color of your outfit was meant as a reminder of your past vocation." Oh, Lord! He shouldn't have said that.

Her laugh instantly banished his sour mood. She was sunshine. She was joy. As they wound down the outside stairs, he began to laugh with her.

"I hope you weren't trying to tell me that this outfit reminds you of a religious habit."

"Hardly. There wouldn't be many nuns who remained celibate wearing dresses like that."

"Hmm. Thanks . . . I think."

"You're welcome, I think." He stopped right there under the streetlight in her parking lot and kissed her. Then he seated her in the car and hurried around to the driver's side, anxious not to miss one second of her company.

He led the conversation into general territory, asking her about school and relating a little bit about his business.

"You do have your acceptance speech ready, don't you?"

David laughed at her total conviction that he was

going to win. "No. If I do get the award, I'll wing it."

Before she could comment further, David turned in to the circular drive of one of Atlanta's swankiest hotels. They were about ten cars back from the unloading spot, which was full of sightseers and camera men and photographers.

"Heavens!" Kathlyn exclaimed. "Couldn't you let me out here?"

David laughed and patted her hand. "It'll be fine. You don't have to do anything except smile and hang on to me. Those lights and flashbulbs can be blinding."

Lights. Camera. Action! Kathlyn thought, determined not to panic. She had no idea what she was doing here, but there was no backing out now. She took a deep breath, preparing to exit the car sedately and with dignity. Those people might wonder who she was, but there was no way she was going to look like a foolish hick.

Just as the doorman was reaching for her door, David teased, "Chin up, honey. You're about to be on *Candid Camera.*"

Kathlyn tried to fight her laughter, but lost. She exited the car looking as if she were having the time of her life. David was quick to join her as the attendant sped off with his car. He offered her his arm and guided her forward. It was exactly like the Academy Awards nights she'd seen on television. She squelched an urge to bow her head to the adoring public. She heard the people on the sidelines whispering: "That's Sheila." "No, that's JoAnne." Kathlyn clung tighter to David's arm as they entered double doors that stood open for them.

A maid took her wrap before David led her into the dining room. She scanned the people within her line of vision, and gulped. Directly in front of her was the mayor of Atlanta. Farther to her right was Jeremy Stanton, even more handsome than on the screen. Tearing her gaze away from him, she noticed a highly successful rock singer her students had begged her to listen to. And in the center of all this fame and fortune, here she was—Kathlyn Marie McDaniel, almost-nun and high school teacher.

David kept an eye on her. He watched her scan the room and wondered how she'd react. He hoped she wouldn't go all star-struck and clam up on him.

She giggled. It was a behind-the-hand, trying-to-camouflage-it giggle.

"What's so funny?"

"Life. This." She flung her hand out to encompass their surroundings. "It's marvelous! Thanks for bringing me."

"Thanks for coming." His intuition had been right. She was going to turn this ordeal into something delightful.

"David!" The booming voice was soon followed by a bald, roundish man. "Glad you could make it, old boy. Congratulations on the nomination. Good to have you back where you belong."

"Thanks, James. It's good to be back. I'd like you to meet—"

"Oh, no need to introduce this young lady. She's been in the headlines often lately. It's a pleasure to meet you, Julia."

"Kathlyn," Kathlyn and David corrected simultaneously.

"Right," continued James. "Can't keep y'all straight. Saw you in *Pretty Woman*. So tell me, what is that Gere fellow like?"

Stunned, Kathlyn replied, "Sexy?"

"Figures." The older man sighed deeply. "But it's great to see one of our own Georgia peaches make good. Enjoy your evening, Julia, er, Kathlyn. You, too, David, you lucky son of a gun." And he was off, his booming voice leading the way.

Kathlyn looked at David. David looked at Kathlyn. There was a pregnant pause, and then they shrugged.

"So you find the Gere fellow sexy, huh?"

Kathlyn blushed and nodded.

"And do you find me sexy?" He was fishing, but who cared?

Kathlyn raised her sparkling blue eyes to his. "Oh, yes," she whispered.

David took a big gulp of air. He didn't know if it was right for him to let her feel that way about him. His muddled brain was trying to tell him he was probably leading her on—a nun! But after all his "geeky" years, it still felt good to have his body admired. He turned in answer to an insistent tug on his sleeve.

"Shame on you, David, for keeping this lovely young lady all to yourself. Introduce us."

David smiled at his longtime friend. "Kathlyn, I'd like you to meet Doreen Langston. Doreen, this is Kathlyn."

Doreen raised her eyebrows at David's tone. God, she'd have given anything to have him say her name with that touch of reverence. She turned and looked at Kathlyn. *Stunning. Intelligent. A sense of humor. And falling in love with David St. John. Poor dear. Doesn't she know how hopeless that is?*

Doreen turned back to David and saw a look of confusion. *Confusion? David? Goodness. Things might just be getting very interesting around here.*

"It's a pleasure to meet you. Kathlyn." She shook Kathlyn's hand.

"The pleasure is all mine." Kathlyn was trying not to sound awestruck. It was easier if she thought about this stunning movie star wearing braces on her teeth. It was almost simple when she remembered the hurt this woman had caused David in high school.

"Heavens," Doreen said, raising her hand to her generous, overflowing breasts. "What did I do to cause that scowl? David, what have you been telling her about me?"

"Just that you ruined my high school prom."

"Me ruin yours? I'm afraid he has that backwards, Kathlyn. I suppose he told you how he ran out and saved my virtue from that bully of a quarterback? How he kicked the guy in the back of the knee while I was in his arms?"

"Well . . ."

"Well, nothing. It's all a lie." Doreen was indignant, but Kathlyn could tell she was having fun with David. "I had everything under control. I only wanted to see what it was like to kiss the boy. Trouble was, after the kiss, I laid my head on his chest, and my braces got stuck on a button thread. When David knocked the guy down, I had to topple right along with him or have my teeth jerked out of my head.

"When my mother saw the condition of my formal, she was rather upset. Poor David took the brunt of my mother's tirade and didn't say a word. After she'd calmed down and I'd explained the whole thing to her, she thought David was a knight in shining armor. Still does, poor, deluded woman."

She patted David's cheek and exclaimed, "Oh, there's Jeremy! Must go, darlings. See you later." She was gone in a puff of chiffon and Obsession.

"Curiouser and curiouser," Kathlyn muttered.

David just grinned. Another couple came up to them, and then another and another.

The funniest thing kept happening. When David introduced Kathlyn, he was always interrupted before he could say her last name.

"Kathlyn, darling," a woman crooned. "We've heard so much about you and wanted to introduce ourselves. Margaret and Charles Larwing. It's a pleasure to finally meet you."

By this time, Kathlyn had simply given up. She took the lady's hand graciously. "The pleasure is mine, Margaret." Kathlyn bowed her head to the gentleman. "Charles."

"Ms. Kathlyn," the man said with wonder in his voice, "I'm so glad to make your acquaintance."

The couple left, and Kathlyn glared at David.

"I swear I haven't the foggiest idea what's going on," he said.

David held out a pink-cushioned dining chair and motioned her to be seated. "I told you, you looked like a movie star or a model." He squinted his eyes, studying her. "However, I still think you favor Lauren Hutton much more than Julia Roberts . . . though maybe you're a cross between them."

Their other dinner companions joined them. Each couple greeted David and repeated how happy they were to make Kathlyn's acquaintance. She looked at a grinning David and rolled her eyes.

Throughout the meal, the other couples teased David about the possibility of the federal government coming after him for accumulating so many companies. They all sounded slightly in awe of him, wondering how he could possibly manage so many companies. David only smiled and explained that the task wasn't impossible. But his smile did not reach his eyes. There was no hint of the sparkle they'd held after his trip to the paper mill.

"Have you visited each company you own?" she asked him when the others settled down to eat.

"Some. I've hired competent people to explain the status of a failing business. We then have one of our interminable meetings and decide if we should take them on."

Oh, yes. He'd definitely prefer being out in the field doing the research.

Just as the conversation was getting around to Kathlyn, the mayor rapped loudly on his table and got everyone's attention. He gave out a number of civic awards to deserving people and then turned the meeting over to the president of the chamber of commerce.

The man spoke fluently and eloquently about David. Even though he had brought his business to their city only a few months ago, he had taken several local businesses from the edge of bankruptcy into prosperity and kept many of Atlanta's citizens employed. He'd also donated and endorsed many of the city's charitable organizations, helping the poor and needy when the system let them slip through the cracks.

When David's name was called to come forward to receive the Man of the Year award, Kathlyn wanted to stand up and cheer. When he rejoined her, she put her arms around his neck and kissed him.

And felt his anger.

Surprised, she moved back and looked deeply into his eyes. He turned away from her. Didn't he like receiving awards? Surely he didn't feel undeserving.

He accepted congratulations from others. He was polite and courteous, but not the outgoing, easygoing David she knew.

Soon he maneuvered them toward the exit. Before

Kathlyn realized it, they were standing outside the hotel waiting for the car to be brought around.

He didn't say anything, even after they were heading home. David's hands were white where they gripped the steering wheel.

"What's the matter?"

He jumped at the sound of her voice. "Nothing!"

"Right."

"I said nothing was the matter!"

Kathlyn settled back in her seat and looked straight ahead.

"Listen, I don't need some confused religious fanatic trying to figure out what's wrong with me."

Kathlyn held her silence. He was obviously frustrated and angry.

After another mile or so, he finally exploded. "Okay, there is something wrong! Does that make you feel better?"

"No."

"Good, because I'm mad as hell. I didn't deserve that award. I despise people going on and on about the charities and good works others have done. For God's sake, I didn't do any of it for a slap on the back. I also didn't move to Atlanta to make the city more prosperous or to help lower unemployment. It was a sound business decision. Atlanta is more central to the country and my businesses. I grew up here. I wanted to come home. Just damn them. Damn them all to hell!"

Kathlyn winced, but said nothing.

They made it to her parking lot in record time. He shut off the engine and turned toward her.

"I'm not a saint, Kathlyn. In fact, I'm probably headed in the other direction. I'm tired of the job I do. I want to be out in the field helping companies and small businesspeople. Or maybe doing something else entirely. I want to throw up my hands and let everyone involved fend for themselves. I think half the companies I have could have survived without my help, but the owners were too lazy to take the initiative and try to run them. I feel like I'm being used. I don't feel like a saint who deserves that award. And damn it all, I want to take you to bed and make love to you until we've both finally had enough!''

He turned forward, stared out the window, and then banged his hand hard against the steering wheel.

Kathlyn's heart was beating like crazy from the barrage of emotions coming from him. She wanted to help him, soothe him, do anything to make his world right again, but felt helpless.

''Thanks for the evening,'' she said softly, and reached for the door handle.

''That's all the hell you have to say?''

''What do you want? Do you want me to tell you to go ahead and sell those companies? To find someone else who does if the former owners don't want them? Mention that I've never seen you happier than when you returned from your trip to Portland? You know all that.

''If you want me to tell you that I'll go to bed with you, I won't. You knew that before you asked me out tonight. If you want me to admit that I want you as much as you want me, I will. But I won't go to bed with you.'' *And as for getting enough of you? That could very well be impossible.*

Kathlyn let herself out of the car and walked away. She heard a car door slam, and his angry footsteps following her.

''Don't you dare walk away from me like that!'' He caught up with her and, grabbing her by the shoulders, turned her toward him. ''Don't.'' His voice cracked, and he hauled her into his arms. He squeezed tightly, desperately.

Poor man. Why couldn't he admit that he needed her? Needed someone to hold on to. She put her head on his shoulder and held him. He rocked her gently. He kissed her hair and whispered, "I'm sorry."

His body stiffened, and he pulled away from her. He couldn't even apologize without feeling uncomfortable about it.

"Let me spend the night."

"I don't think that's a good idea."

"I'll be good," he promised, but the devil was beginning to lurk through the shadows in his eyes. "I'll stay on the couch like last time, and you can lull me to sleep with the cello."

She began to shake her head when she heard his reluctant "Please?"

She sighed. She took his hand and led him up the stairs.

Once inside, he took off his tuxedo jacket and undid the studs at the cuffs of the starched white shirt. He rolled up his sleeves and went into her minuscule kitchen to make coffee, just as if he were at home.

"Why don't you change into something more comfortable?" He wiggled his eyebrows.

Kathlyn chuckled all the way down the hallway to her bedroom. What a night! And what a tangle this relationship was becoming. If David was the one intended to be her mate, the road leading to marriage was certainly going to be very rocky.

She sighed as she stepped out of her shoes and peeled down her panty hose. With only a moment's hesitation, she slipped into a modest, flowing, multicolored caftan. When she entered the living room, David's frown disappeared. He'd poured the coffee and was seated on the couch.

"Join me." He patted the spot next to him.

Considering that that same spot would soon be used as his bed, Kathlyn opted for the rocking chair.

"Chicken."

Kathlyn nodded agreement. She knew she'd be putty in his hands if he touched her, and after what she'd revealed in the car—about wanting him—she figured he would very much want to touch her.

"So, how often do you have trouble sleeping?" It was a guess on her part.

"I never said . . ."

Kathlyn simply raised her eyebrow. That move did come in handy.

"All right. Most nights. There's always so much on my mind. It won't shut down."

"What?"

"This and that."

"This to do, or that you'd like to do?"

He leaned over and picked up his coffee cup from the table in front of him. He took a sip before answering. "More *that* I'd like to do, but it's also become *this* I should be doing."

"How long has this been going on?"

"A little over a year, now. But, hey, I've got it good. I still accomplish mountains of things. You heard the chamber president rattling on. It's just . . ." He frowned and sipped the coffee. "It's just that I think I could be doing more, accomplishing more. I guess it's time to stop procrastinating and set this overworked brain to finding the solution."

He put his coffee cup back on the table with a definite thump and rose to his feet. "Anything you want to get out of the bathroom before I use it?"

End of conversation. Kathlyn shook her head and rose to get the bed linens.

When she returned, she handed David the bedding and went into the bathroom to wash her face and brush her teeth. What a complex man. But what a dear one. He was exciting and tender and, oh, so many things.

She returned to the living room to find David lying on the couch, his hands behind his head, the blue sheet pulled up to his navel. That glorious chest she'd seen last time he'd slept over drew her eyes and made her fingertips itch. She'd never felt a man's chest hair. Was it soft or bristly? It looked like swirls of hot fudge topping on his peanut butter toffee skin.

She locked her door and turned out the kitchen light. She then went to the statue and ran a gentle hand over the folds of the plaster of Paris veil. "Good night," she whispered.

"Why do you talk to statues?" He sounded curious.

"I talk to the people they represent. This one of Jesus' mother is one of my favorites. I talk to her a lot."

"Is rubbing your hand over it superstitious?"

She rubbed the statue one more time and then came closer to David. "No. It's a tactile thing. I like to touch it to remind me that Mary is real, not some fantasy spirit floating around somewhere. That statue has been a part of my life for a long time. It holds a lot of memories."

"Sit down, Kathlyn." He patted the spot next to his hip. "Tell me about your life."

This time she seated herself next to him. She wanted him to understand how deep her convictions were.

"I told you that my parents were Scottish and Irish— good Catholic stock. Their faith was marvelous. They walked around talking to God all the time. Their faith

and the church were the backbones of their lives. The
foundation of their marriage.

"My dad died when I was ten, and Mom went to
work for our pastor in St. Louis as his housekeeper.
We lived only two doors from the rectory. One day,
when I was a freshman in high school, Mom suddenly
took ill. Within twenty-four hours she was dead. Some
people question God when something like that happens.
Because of my upbringing, I only leaned more heavily
on my faith. Without it, I'm sure I wouldn't have made
it through that terrible time." *Oh, how she still missed
them.*

"I had no idea what was going to happen to me. I
was only fifteen, and I guess I could have been turned
over to the courts."

"You had no other family?"

"No. The religious sisters who taught at the parish
grade school and high school had their own residence.
A convent. They took me in. I had my own room, and
I wound up with twelve mothers instead of one."

Kathlyn laughed softly. "It made for some interesting times. The sisters encouraged me to have friends
over just like in an ordinary home. We used to play
hide-and-seek in the chapel. One night we even bor-
rowed a couple of their old habits and tried them on at
a friend's house.

"The sisters put their foot down when they caught
some of my friends smoking in the bathroom, but Father Tom told me that if I was going to sneak around
doing it anyway, I could smoke on his screened
porch."

"Did you? I never would have lit one there."

"Once, just to try it. Why wouldn't you?"

"Because the few priests I've seen have scared the
hell out of me."

Between guffaws, Kathlyn said, "That's their job, David."

"Scaring people is their job?"

"No, scaring the hell out of them."

"Cute. Did you date while you were in high school?"

"Well, of course—a little. I wasn't a prissy recluse."

"So it seems."

"Most boys had a bit of a problem with picking me up and taking me home to the convent, but a few were brave enough to do it. And only one got caught trying to kiss me. Poor Sister Angelica. I think she was more embarrassed than Peter was.

"Are you going to pry the whole story out of me tonight?" she asked with a sigh.

"Yes."

"Then let me heat up the coffee. You want some?"

"Thanks. I'll get it."

"Don't move!" Kathlyn exclaimed as David began to lift the sheet.

He laughed and reached over to grab his shirt.

When Megan returned with the steaming mugs, David had put on his shirt but had not replaced the studs. That was fine with her. She liked looking at his muscled, hair-swirled chest, a lot more of which was exposed now that he was sitting up, with his back against the couch's arm.

"We were up to the part where you finished high school and went into the convent."

"No, after high school I went on to college. My parents had left a trust fund for my education, but not enough to board. I went to a nearby Catholic college and continued to live with the sisters. During my fourth year I finally made the decision to enter the convent. I was sure God was calling me to the religious life.

"After I got my degree, I entered the Convent of the Sisters of Mercy. I taught at one of their affiliated schools during my postulancy—a time of adjustment. A sampling of religious life. After six months I donned the white veil of the novitiate. That's a trial period. A time to examine yourself and see if you have a true calling.

"Usually the novices take temporary vows after two or three years. The closer I came to taking the vows, the more I had doubts. Halfway through that second year, I went back for a visit to the little convent I grew up in. I spent long hours in front of my statue, talking to Mary, praying to God for guidance."

"What did you have doubts about?"

"I was okay on the vows of poverty and obedience. It's just that every time I thought about taking the vow of chastity, I felt such a deep loss, felt that something in me would not be fulfilled.

"Finally I talked to Sister Angelica. She let me ramble on and didn't say a word until I said, 'But I have this strong faith. Surely God wants me to be a sister.'

"Do you know what she did then? She laughed and said, 'My dear child! Are you trying to tell me that you think only those in religious orders have strong faiths?'

"I thought about my parents and the many friends I had who loved their faith and went to church because they wanted to, not because they had to. And finally I knew what God had been telling me every time I thought about permanent chastity. I wanted to share my life with a man. I needed to have children and raise them in the faith."

She quickly drained her coffee cup and got up from the couch. "That was almost two years ago. Sister Angelica found this job for me, so I packed up and left

St. Louis. I'm finding my way in the world and doing what I can for the church.''

''And waiting for a husband.''

David hadn't realized that he'd spoken the thought out loud until she stopped on her way to the kitchen and looked back at him with serious blue eyes.

''Yes.''

He cleared his throat. ''And if he never comes?''

She continued on to the kitchen. ''Don't be silly. Of course he will.''

David couldn't figure out just how she knew that so certainly. Here he was, fumbling around in his career, and God had supposedly given him an extra supply of brains. And there she was, knowing exactly where she was going in life. Somehow that didn't seem fair.

She came back and kissed him on the forehead. ''Good night, David. Sweet dreams.''

''Huh? Oh, sweet dreams to you too, angel. Thanks for talking.''

''You're welcome. Perhaps someday you'll do the same.''

''Perhaps.'' His frown turned into a grin. ''Now go to bed. I'm exhausted.''

She shuffled down the hallway to her room, chuckling. He scooted down on the couch and rested his arms under his head on the pillow. What would it be like to have a faith such as hers? To believe so strongly in something without concrete proof? He used to go to church and Sunday school. He couldn't remember why he had stopped. He only knew that at some point in his life, he'd turned to logical thinking rather than accepting on blind faith. His faith had always been in himself, in his ability to reason and figure out the whys. The thought of accepting a faith wasn't repugnant to him, though. In fact, after getting to know Kathlyn, he thought that it wouldn't be so bad to give himself a break and stop questioning everything. Could he do that? He didn't know. Perhaps he'd try it. Someday.

Right now, however, he'd better figure out what to do with his career. It had certainly been brought home to him tonight that he couldn't go on the way he was. He was not fulfilling himself. He was merely spinning his wheels in success.

He suddenly started laughing.

"What's so funny?" came the inquiry from the bedroom.

"Nothing. I thought you were going to sleep."

"I was, almost, until someone started laughing like a lunatic."

"I was not. And if you can't sleep, you can come out here and keep me company on this couch."

"Good night, David."

He chuckled under his breath. Got her that time. Trouble was, that little wisp of a woman had gotten him, too. Not that he wouldn't have figured out what to do with all those companies he owned. Not that he had needed her suggestion to sell them. He had gotten most of them on solid footing. They would definitely be snapped up.

That was it! He wasn't exactly sure what he wanted to do, but it definitely was not to accumulate companies. He needed something that would quench his thirst for knowledge and help people at the same time.

He jumped off the couch and hurried, in briefs only, into Kathlyn's room, where he smacked a big kiss on her lips.

"David St. John!"

"Go to sleep, angel."

He left the room and headed right to the statue. He patted it on the head and whispered, "Good night."

He turned off the lamp next to the couch and climbed under the sheet. He fluffed up the pillow, lay down on it, and, still smiling, shut his eyes.

The smile disappeared and his eyes popped open again. *I want you as much as you want me. Waiting for a husband? Yes.*

"Damn!"

FIVE

Coffee! David's nostrils twitched, and his taste buds awoke. Kathlyn was moving around in the kitchen, but he lay on the couch, trying to regroup his thoughts. He had to talk to her, but what was he going to say? As a member of Mensa, surely he could put the right words together.

Making sure she was still in the kitchen, he rose and grabbed his pants on the way to the bathroom. Having delayed as long as he could, he finally took a deep breath and went to join her.

"Good morning." Her low, sexy voice made goose bumps rise on David's skin. The man who married her would probably be late for work every morning.

"Morning." He quickly headed to the kitchen for a fortifying cup of coffee.

"I could make you some eggs, if you'd like."

"Thanks, but coffee's fine." He joined her at the round table and set his mug on the blue, woven mat in front of him. "You don't have to rush off, do you?"

"No. I have all day." He looked so good, so scrumptious, sitting there in his open dress shirt. She wanted to touch his chest and run her fingers through his curly head of hair. Lord, he looked good in the morning, stubble and all. She smiled as she noticed that his hair needed trimming. She felt like reminding him— as a wife would. She reigned in her thoughts.

"After our conversation last night," David said, "I figured I'd better explain something to you. The things I said the first night we met? Well, I meant every one of them."

"You did?"

"Yeah, but usually it's just one of my approaches."

"Does it ever work?"

"I know it sounds unbelievable, but yes. Sometimes. Actually, it breaks the ice, and lets an interested lady know where we're going."

"And if that fails?"

"Well, then I try a slower approach."

"Was that what you were doing with me?"

"I thought so. But every time I was with you, I did what came naturally instead of using any techniques."

"What came naturally worked just fine. For a while there I was worried that you could make me go to bed with you without my knowing what was happening."

"You wouldn't have given yourself without love and marriage."

He reached over and clasped her left hand, loving the feel of it resting in his, rubbing his thumb over the calluses she'd developed playing the cello.

"Listen, angel. I'm not going to be the husband you're waiting for. I have this problem with being in a relationship for the long haul. I don't jump from bed to bed, but . . . I'll never marry."

Kathlyn felt an odd twisting in her stomach. Why? She barely knew David. Surely she had not had her heart set on marrying him. Then why this acute disappointment?

She looked into his eyes and was shocked at what she saw. He had believed his words, but his beautiful, sad eyes could not disguise the pain of wishing they were not true.

"How can you be so certain?"

"I just am, okay?" He sounded angry, unwilling to talk about it anymore. As she watched, he ran his hand agitatedly through his hair, and rose to pace the small area.

"The thing is . . ." He came to stand in front of her and ran his long, lean finger along her cheek. "The thing is, angel, I really enjoy being with you. Even knowing that my rampaging hormones can't be satisfied with you, I want to be with you. It's as if there is a bond, a chemistry joining us. Could we . . ." He dropped his hand and cleared his throat. "Could we possibly be friends?"

Kathlyn released the breath she had been holding. She had thought he was going to say they could not see each other anymore. Her anguish at that thought disappeared, and her heart beat once again with joy. "Yes, we most definitely can."

He smiled. She nearly swooned. She wanted to run her fingers along those parentheses at the sides of his mouth. She wanted to kiss him, not as a friend, but as they had the other night—tongues, lips, breath, all mingling.

As if reading her thoughts, he brought his mouth down to hers. "One last time, angel."

She opened her lips immediately, tasting the heady flavors of coffee, mouthwash, and David. Her knees went weak, and when David lifted her from the chair, she latched her arms around his neck. Her breasts seemed to sizzle as they came in contact with his solid chest. Her tongue explored, savored, dueled with his. And she felt a dampness between her legs, the heady, reckless feeling of arousal.

When he lifted his head and tightened his arms around her, her head flopped against his shoulder. She didn't even realize that her fingers were still playing in the curls at the back of his neck until he took her hands and brought them to his mouth.

"Friends." His voice was hoarse. "From now on, God help me, no more of this." He gave her a quick peck on the cheek and stepped back, releasing her hands.

Kathlyn felt chilled at the loss of the heat of his body. Her own arousal cooled, a little. She looked up at him and smiled. "From now on, just friends. But thanks for the kiss."

"You're welcome." His grin was almost irresistible. She clenched her hands into fists and turned toward the kitchen. "Sure you don't want some breakfast?"

Yeah. I'd love to have breakfast. You sprawled beneath me in your virgin bed. He needed to get away from her. Needed to get his emotions under control. The next time he saw her, he'd have the right attitude about their friendship, but he couldn't stay near her now.

"No, thanks. I have to be going." He walked by her and patted her fanny. A friendly gesture, he assured himself. "I'll see you soon."

"See you soon," she echoed.

David left Kathlyn's apartment delighted. He would still be seeing her, and she understood that marriage would not be in the picture. They were going to do exciting things and have fun—this time without all the sexual tension. He hoped.

But seeing Kathlyn without being able to have her was not exactly his picture of euphoria. Euphoria would be their wonderfully nude bodies rubbing and writhing on cool sheets warmed by the passion they stirred in each other. Euphoria would be the climax they achieved after hours of playing, hours of building the sexual tension—a climax so earth-shattering that both would have trouble returning to reality. He reached for the car door handle with shaking hands and a perspiring body.

Had things been normal, this might have been the start of something lasting, a step toward marriage. He understood his mother's longing for a normal life. However, like her, he'd never been normal. Marriage was not for him.

"You're weird, Davey," his friends had taunted when he had caught a baseball and stopped to examine it instead of throwing it to first for the out. His playmates had thrown him out of the game.

All through school he had been odd man out—weird. He hadn't had many friends. He still didn't.

He got in his car, shaking his head. She probably has lots of friends—guys who would be thrilled to take her out to dinner, romance her, kiss her. He swore and gunned the engine. She'd just better watch out for the fast ones. No, he'd watch out for them. After all, being Kathlyn's friend gave him some rights. The main one he could see right now was that of being protector. Yes, he'd protect her from lechers waiting for innocent virgins to appear on the scene.

All hell broke loose on Sunday. The society section and the business section of the *Atlanta Journal* carried pictures and reports of the awards banquet. The headline in the society section was WHO IS DAVID ST. JOHN'S LATEST? Photos of her and David jumped out at Kathlyn. Everyone, it seemed, wanted to know who the mystery lady was, and why she had not given her last name.

It was all very amusing until the phone calls started coming in. She escaped by spending the day and night at Sandra's house.

That night in a strange bed she cried as she had most of Saturday, reprimanding herself for crying even as the tears fell. But even though she still had David's friendship, she felt as if she had lost something vital to her well-being.

The next morning, refusing to hide, she went to school. The faculty lounge was packed with teachers and aides and administrators, all teasing her and trying to dig out the scoop.

Her first class was chaos. The students wanted to know all. Finally Kathlyn gave up on her lesson plans and told them about all the stars and government muck-a-mucks she had seen, what they had worn, what they had said.

The second class was going much the same way until David walked in. Everyone stopped talking, except for a boy whose back was turned to the door.

"Wonder if he scrumped her." The boy's whispered words shouted into the silence. The class gasped as a whole, Kathlyn blushed beet red, and David said, "You, kid. Out in the hall!"

"Hey, man," the boy blustered, "I ain't gotta go nowhere with you."

"If you want me to call the principal in on this, that's okay with me. Man."

David started toward the door. The boy reluctantly followed.

Furious, David stood with arms crossed over his chest, legs spread in a battle stance. It didn't help that the brazen kid slumped nonchalantly against the beige brick wall next to the closed classroom door. His blond hair was too long, his stubbled chin too belligerent. David looked the kid squarely in the eyes—brown eyes filled with . . . fear?

"You got a girl, kid?"

"Yeah. What's it to you?"

"You scrump her?"

"Yeah, man. She loves it."

"A real tramp, hey?"

The kid moved in a second, fists raised. David grabbed his arms just in time.

"No one calls my old lady a tramp!"

"I hate to disagree with you, but you just did."

"No way, man. My Katie ain't no tramp. She's the sweetest thing ever put on this earth."

"Does she know that you go around calling what you do 'scrumping'?" The kid actually blushed.

"No. She'd kill me if she heard me say that."

"Do you go around telling your buddies what you two do together?"

"Jeez, man, no. Not everything. Hell, a guy's got to live up to his image, don't he?"

"Depends on the image."

"Yeah, well, I had to drop out for a while. I'm twenty, and the guys kind of think of me as a stud, ya know? I've been the dummy for so many years, I had to do something to make up for it."

"So you became the troublemaker, the big tough guy?"

After a few seconds, the kid nodded.

David smiled and let go of the kid's arms. "The name's David St. John."

Again came the blush. "Jerry. Jerry Monroe."

The two eyed each other speculatively, silently.

"Uh, you ain't going to tell the principal this, are you?"

"Depends on you."

"Geez," the kid groaned, riffling a hand through his long hair. "The old lady'd—"

"Kill me." David and Jerry spoke together.

"Yeah," Jerry finished grimly.

"Do you call Katie your old lady?"

"Yeah, and she'd kill me for that, too."

"Bloodthirsty little thing."

Jerry laughed. "No way, man. Like I said, she's the sweetest girl in the whole world. Kind of bossy, though. She's the reason I'm still here in this dumb school instead of full-time at trade school. She says she wants me to get a full-fledged high school diploma, none of that GED stuff. She supports us while I go here during the day and to trade school at night."

"You're married?"

"Yeah. Kind of nice being married to her. Except, of course, when she's bossy."

David could tell that the kid didn't really mind that at all. Good God—twenty and married. But even with all the hardships the couple had to be going through, the kid had a sparkle in his eyes every time he mentioned his Katie.

"Hell, all I want to do is get this diploma and finish the plumbing class at night school so's I can get a job. Katie works at a department store. Never complains, ya know, but I can tell it's hard on her."

"Guess she loves you."

"Yeah. Hard to believe."

"How about you go back in and apologize to Ms. McDaniel?"

"Kind of figured you'd say that. Planned on doing it, anyway." David saw beneath Jerry's tough exterior.

Here was a struggling young man who deserved a chance.

Jerry straightened and put his hand on the doorknob to enter the classroom. He looked over his shoulder.

David spoke. "Why don't you tell your buddies I offered you a job."

Jerry looked at him slyly. "Would I be lying?"

"When do you graduate?"

"May twenty-fourth. I'm passing everything."

"You do drugs? Drink?"

Jerry turned to face David. "No, sir."

David slapped the kid on the shoulder. "You won't be lying about the job." He reached into his pocket and pulled out one of his business cards. "Call me in a couple of days. I'll see what I can line up for you. But remember, I don't put up with any mouthing off."

"I'll remember."

As the two entered the classroom, every eye followed Jerry's march across the room. "Sorry, Ms. McDaniel. It won't happen again."

Kathlyn had been having trouble with Jerry since she'd started teaching. Now, the change in his voice startled her. She'd had no idea he could string two proper words together without a swear word or a *man* between them.

"Thank you, Jerry. Your apology is accepted."

Jerry resumed his seat, but no one dared say anything.

David walked up to Kathlyn and turned his back to the class. "I came to apologize for the things that were said in the paper."

She stepped a little to the side. "Class, get out something to study." She stepped back so that David once again blocked her. She looked at him in his gorgeous dark blue suit and tie and sparkling white shirt, and had to shove her hands into the pockets of her gray linen pants to keep from touching him. Her gray and white checked jacket and short-sleeved cotton blouse, so comfortable only moments before, were suddenly unbearably hot.

She cleared her throat before she spoke again. "You had nothing to do with that fiasco the other night. We tried to tell them my last name. Except for the uncomfortable stir it's causing, the whole thing is rather funny."

"Are you all right? I tried to call you all day yesterday. I even went by your apartment, but you weren't home."

He was looking so closely at her, he could probably see the flush she felt in her cheeks. "I went undercover at a friend's house. And yes, I'm fine."

She felt the pleasure of his nearness too acutely, so she moved away and addressed the class. "Students, I'd like you to meet my friend David St. John."

"Hello, Mr. St. John," the class recited like kindergartners. Everyone laughed.

"Ask him to the prom, Ms. McDaniel," one of the girls piped up softly.

Kathlyn felt her face burn hotter. "I . . ."

"You're the one who told us to ask the guy we wanted to go with." The implication was that Kathlyn would be out of her mind if she didn't.

Kathlyn surrendered. She turned to David. "If you have nothing to do this coming Saturday night, would you like to chaperon the senior prom with me?"

"Yes, Ms. McDaniel."

The students applauded. Under the noise David whispered, "Chaperoning the prom should be a heck of a lot easier than attending my own."

"Don't count on it," Kathlyn said with a knowing smile.

Later that evening Kathlyn searched through her closet, hoping that she'd find something to wear to the prom other than the black dress she had worn to the awards banquet. There was nothing else.

She sat down at her desk and brought out her checkbook and savings account statements. Neither was ever healthy, but they had seldom been quite this sickly. She scanned the entries. A check for the dance lessons she had taken so she could teach the students for the concert. Checks for food, rent, and utilities. Donations to the church, and gifts for her CCD class. It all added up. It all subtracted correctly. Her savings account had also shrunk to where she could feel the pinch. A summer job was all that would keep her afloat.

Her job from last summer was no longer available. Mr. Sarentini had had to put his out-of-work son-in-law on the payroll of the family-owned grocery store. He could not afford to hire Kathlyn, too. She'd been searching in vain for something else, and wishing every day that she had gone into another field of education. Music teachers weren't needed for summer school. She *could* advertise for music students for private lessons, but that might not bring in enough to cover her bills. She shrugged away the thought for now. Something would come up. But one thing was sure—she was going to go to the prom in that same black dress. David could think what he liked.

He arrived at six-thirty on Saturday night. They planned to go out to eat and then arrive at the dance ahead of the students. Kathlyn's heart flipped when she saw David. It happened every time she saw him. He was such a handsome man. How could she resist?

He didn't say anything about her dress. In fact, his eyes filled with the identical fire they had the last time she'd worn it. As she basked in the warmth of the look, she warned herself about playing with fire. The flames were not frightening, she told herself, only mesmerizing.

David had made reservations for dinner at the inn where the prom was to be held. He thought they could share a relaxing meal and linger over their after-dinner drinks before having to go to work. The dining room, though, was half-filled with students and their dates. They all greeted Kathlyn and David. He could hear some speculating about how serious it was between them.

Youth, David thought. The girls were all swooning romantics, and the boys were collections of hyperactive hormones. A few more years and . . . He looked at Kathlyn. A few more years and the girls would still be romantics, and the boys would be men who were satisfying their lust having "meaningful affairs."

"What do we do now?" David asked as he and Kathlyn took up their positions at the hallway entrance leading to the ballroom.

"Collect tickets and make sure that once a couple enters the prom, they don't leave unless they're not going to return."

"Why can't they come back in?"

"Rules. It's the best way we can figure out to keep them from going out into the parking lot and drinking."

Not bad, David thought as he took up his post next to Kathlyn and watched her collect tickets. Each couple greeted her with big smiles and eyed him speculatively. He grinned back at them, and watched as the girls blushed and the boys hustled their dates a little faster past him.

As the line grew, David moved across from Kathlyn and began collecting tickets. Some time after the crush, a lone couple wandered in. David could tell that the young man had already been drinking, and could see the anger on his date's face. As they moved past him, he noticed the bulge in the guy's hip pocket. The girl detoured into the ladies' room, and the young man headed toward the men's. David followed.

He held out his hand. "I'll take the flask."

The kid backed away from David. "Hey, I'm twenty-one."

David followed like a shadow. "Makes no difference in here. The rules say no alcohol allowed at the prom."

The young man handed the flask over to David with an angry shove. "I didn't want to come to this damn dance, anyway. I hate dancing."

"So why're you here?"

"Because Crissy wanted to come. Girls like all this dancing and romantic stuff. Dressing in this monkey suit makes me feel like a fool."

"Crissy was angry with you when you arrived, right? If I know women, she's in the ladies' room crying."

The young man actually looked ashamed. Then he straightened his spine and looked belligerently at David. "What difference can it make? She's not going to have a good time either way. What fun is going to a prom and standing around watching the others dance?"

David remembered his senior prom, remembered standing around watching Doreen dance with everyone but him. "Not much. I know."

"*Sure* you do."

David walked over to the sink and slowly poured the Jack Daniels down the drain. Without turning around, he said, "I wouldn't think it takes much to get out on the dance floor these days. Seems like they all shuffle their feet to the slow ones and jerk their bodies around to the fast ones. I've never tried the fast ones, but if my date for the evening wants to, I think I'll give it a try."

"You'd make a fool of yourself." There was no doubt in the kid's voice.

"So, who'd notice?"

David looked into the mirror at the young man's reflection. "You'd be more of a fool sloppy drunk, don't you think?"

"Yeah," the kid admitted reluctantly.

"You could get out and shuffle your feet to the slow ones. Might fulfill Crissy's wish for a romantic evening."

"You think so?"

"Yeah."

David handed the empty flask back. The kid looked at it for a moment and then dropped it into the waste receptacle.

"I thought you had deserted me," Kathlyn said when he rejoined her.

"No, just had to wash my hands. Do we have to stand here all night?"

"No. We've been relieved. Let's go see how the juniors decorated the hall." She linked her arm with David's, and they strolled into the ballroom.

The lights were romantically dim, a rotating crystal ball sprinkling glittering fairy lights over the tuxedoed young men and princesslike young ladies. The floor was crowded with couples slow-dancing, and the band played softly in the background. Balloons decorated the entire front of the bandstand. One corner of the room was filled with a line of students waiting their turn to have their pictures taken. A sign proclaiming the theme of the prom filled an entire wall: FRIENDS FOREVER.

David asked, "Do you think they'll stay friends?"

"Some will. Some'll move on, forget or be forgotten."

David thought about high school. He couldn't remember too many friends. He did remember his college days—taking the time and making the effort to fit in, to be himself and yet be one of the guys. He had made friends, but had not bothered to continue the friendships after graduation. Perhaps it wasn't too late to renew them.

"David? Yoo-hoo, David?"

He snapped out of his reverie and saw Kathlyn's hand waving in front of his face. She laughed and took his arm again. "Let's check all the little nooks and crannies for necking couples."

"Oh, come on, Kathlyn," he pleaded playfully, "let's find our own little corner and do some necking ourselves."

"Behave, David. We have to set a good example."

"We would. They could learn something from the way we'd neck."

Kathlyn laughed her low, spine-tingling laugh and led David around the sidelines. She stopped once and pointed toward the dance floor. "Isn't that couple dancing awfully close?"

The young man from the bathroom had taken David at his word. The couple was on the floor, not shuffling, but swaying to the slow beat of the music. David wasn't sure who was holding whom, but the girl's starry-eyed look told David that she didn't mind the ineptitude of her date's dancing. "No, leave them alone."

"But, David—"

"Kathlyn, just let them be."

She gave him a puzzled look but said no more.

Half an hour passed while Kathlyn and David walked

the perimeter, another while they took their turn at the punch bowl. David thought that they were really there to make sure the stuff didn't get spiked. The way the punch tasted, he was tempted to do it himself. After that duty, they checked the bathrooms.

David laughed when he reentered the ballroom. The music had gradually gotten louder and the tempo faster. He looked over the gyrating couples and saw the young man from the bathroom waving his arms and jerking his body along with the rest of the kids. His date was laughing joyously.

"Mr. St. John," a voice yelled above the strident chords of the music. David looked to his right and saw Jerry.

"It's good to see you," he said.

"I'd like you to meet my Katie." There was pride in Jerry's voice. "Katie, this is Mr. St. John."

"It's a pleasure to meet you." Katie's smile was as sweet as heather. She was five two at the most, and had brown, wavy hair that fell like a cloud around her oval face.

"It's a real pleasure to meet you, Katie. Jerry has mentioned you numerous times."

Katie gave Jerry a sideways glance, and Jerry coughed and stammered. "Good stuff, Katie. Honest."

David came to Jerry's rescue. "Yes, all good."

"Thank you," she said sweetly. "If you'll excuse me, I have to go to the ladies' room."

"Almost got me in trouble there," Jerry said while watching Katie leave the room.

"Sorry. I'm also sorry that I didn't return your call."

"Hey, that's all right, man. You don't owe me anything."

"Knock off the bull," David said sharply. "I told you I'd get you a job, and I meant it. I did some checking on you and talked to the shop teacher and your technical school advisor.''

David saw Jerry swallow hard. "You have talent, kid. You can fix just about anything that breaks. With a few simple instructions, which you're not always ready to listen to, you can do anything you set your mind and hands to doing.''

"Yeah, well, I don't always like people telling me what to do. I've gotten better at listening, though. It's more embarrassing having to go back and ask for those instructions again.''

"Glad to hear it, because I do have something for you.''

"Oh, God." His hands were shaking, so he shoved them into his pockets.

"The deal's off if you don't graduate.''

"I will.''

"Good, because I think you and Katie are going to like this. The best maintenance man I know is getting ready to retire. He handles all the work at The Towers, an apartment complex on the north side. He's agreed to stay on long enough to train you to take over for him. You'd start off at eighteen thousand a year, with a free apartment at The Towers. When Hank retires, your pay would naturally go up.''

"Naturally." Jerry swallowed hard. His face was flushed with excitement. His eyes filled with moisture.

"I also have a job for Katie, if she wants it. Hank's wife has managed the apartments, collecting rent, showing vacancies to new renters. She'll retire with Hank. Katie can have her job on a trial basis, same as yours.''

Jerry wet his lips and reached out a steadier hand to David. "You're looking at the hardest-working maintenance man you'll ever meet. Thanks.''

"You're welcome. Call the office on Monday. Line it up with Hank.

"Wonder what's taking Katie so long?" David said to give the kid a chance to gain control of his emotions.

"She'll be back soon."

"I think you'd better hold on to that one, Jerry."

"I intend to."

David left Jerry and walked out onto the balcony. He stared straight ahead at the gardens laid out before him, lit one of his rare cigarettes and thought about Jerry, making love with the same woman until he was eighty. Or ninety. Or through eternity. Damn it! Here he was, rich as Croesus, with a mind capable of almost anything, and he was envious of a kid who'd barely made it through high school.

Sure he'd had affairs, even tried to stretch some out longer so they would seem more like a marriage, but they had only been sexual. What else could they have been, with him knowing they could never lead to a permanent commitment?

But Kathlyn was . . . home and family, rocking in chairs on a porch well into the next century.

She'd be with her husband that long. She'd still be loving him and filling his life with beauty. She'd give a man something to get up for when he was eighty. When he was eighty, he'd be alone, while the vultures fought over his money.

David sensed her presence before she spoke. "I didn't know you smoked."

"I'm trying to quit." He stubbed out the cigarette on the wall of the balcony. "I'm almost there." Not that it would matter if he lived longer. He didn't see how it would matter to anyone.

"You're in a deep funk. Something I can help you with?"

"No." He couldn't help but smile at her. She was such a joy to look at. "I'm just thinking. My mind has a way of continually working." He took her arm and led her back inside the air-conditioned room. "Will you still be my friend when I'm eighty?"

"I'll still be your friend when we're both floating around in heaven."

David laughed as a picture flashed through his mind of Kathlyn walking beside him with her wings wrapped around his body. It was comforting to think that she'd give up flying to walk with him.

"Let's dance," she said, and led him to the dance floor. The music was dreamy and slow. They melted together as if they had been dancing all their lives. She rested her head on his shoulder, and his arm contracted around her, bringing her close. She smelled of wildflowers and sunshine. She felt like life.

David lost himself in the feel of her. He forgot his dreary thoughts. All he wanted to do was keep her by his side as his friend, forever. She was an angel. He wanted to protect her while she spent time here on earth.

Later, David returned from a bathroom check and halted abruptly in the ballroom. There, in the middle of the floor with the students gathered around to watch, his angel danced. The place was rocking to a forties boogie-woogie, and Kathlyn was going at it down and dirty. She shimmied and shook and jitterbugged. Her hips swayed, making the black satin layers of her dress swirl and tangle. Her shoulders dipped and rolled while light reflected off the crystal ball and sparked like lightning off the sequined bodice of her dress. She held her partner's outstretched hand and circled, a finger shaking in the air, legs moving, hips twisting. So help him, if that kid tossed her in the air like that again, David was going to punch him. Instead, as a finale, the guy bounced Kathlyn on first one knee and then the other.

David was in a sweat. His visions of walking with her and of wings vanished. They were replaced by images of the two of them working up a completely different kind of sweat. With all that energy, she'd be one hell of a partner in bed. With those mile-long legs wrapped around him, he would move in her, she would move with him.

The dance ended. The students clapped and whistled. Kathlyn laughed breathlessly, and David grabbed her for the next dance. He didn't do fast numbers. He didn't rock like the kids did. But his feet moved, his body jerked. Kathlyn laughed and gyrated every part of her body to the driving bass rhythm. It was primitive. He felt primitive. An angel? No, a temptress.

David's heart pounded and his loins ached, but he kept moving with her. Dancing, he knew not how. When the music ended, he was on fire. Kathlyn laughed loudly and exuberantly, and David's teeth ground together to keep from telling her that he wanted to throw her down on the floor, right there in front of the entire student body, and make love to her.

He had to do something, so he took her into his arms and swung her around in a circle, hoping his manhood would retract enough for him to make an unembarrassing exit. When it did, he excused himself and walked back out onto the balcony to light another cigarette. It was impossible to fight all of his vices at the same time.

"Hey, man, you were even worse than I was out there."

David turned to see the kid who'd brought in the flask standing beside him. His words caught David off guard and made him laugh. "You're probably the only one who noticed."

The kid started to say something, then evidently thought better of it. "Yeah, probably. Anyway, I came out here to thank you for what you did. I had a great time without the booze. My girl did, too. Name's Frank Lamont."

David took the outstretched hand in his and shook it. "David St. John."

After Frank had left, Kathlyn came up to David. "How about the last dance?"

"It would be a pleasure, Ms. McDaniel." He wanted to thank Kathlyn for inviting him. The incidents with Jerry and Frank had made him feel good—his presence had made a difference.

"Mr. St. John?" A sexy but sweet female voice interrupted their walk to the dance floor. David turned and saw Katie and Jerry standing beside him.

She stood on tiptoes and kissed him gently on the cheek. "Thank you." Her smile was glowing.

"You're welcome, Katie dear. I take it you plan to accept the manager's position?"

"Yes, sir." She grinned. "It'd be hard to turn down bossing Jerry around."

David looked at Jerry, who was shaking his head at Katie. The kid was so damn much in love with her, and she with him, that David couldn't look at them too long.

"What was that all about?" Kathlyn asked when they were on the dance floor.

David pulled her in closer to him. "Nothing. I just found them jobs."

Kathlyn looked up at David's face, but he pushed her head back down on his shoulder. He didn't want her to see how deeply he wished that couple would make it. Even as skeptical as he was, David couldn't see them being happy with anyone else.

Just then he realized what they were dancing to—"The Wind Beneath My Wings." Katie was Jerry's support. Kathlyn had her God and her saints. He tightened his arms around her and rested his cheek against her cloud of sweet-smelling, blond hair. Sometimes it was hell being so self-sufficient.

SIX

"All right, Kathlyn Marie McDaniel, you got me into this mess. You are going to help me out of it!"

It was midnight, three weeks and three days after that glorious prom. David hadn't called. He hadn't stopped over. The weeks, although busy with end-of-the-year schoolwork, had been lonely. She'd missed David's wacky mood shifts, missed his kisses, missed how complete she felt when he was near.

Now here he stood, looking . . . wonderful. His eyes were bloodshot, his hair badly in need of a trim, and his eyebrows were meeting in a scowl.

"Hi, David." She wanted to wring his neck. She wanted to kiss him. "Won't you come in?"

"Hell, yes, I'll come in. I told you, I need your help. I just hope you haven't signed up for a million things to do this summer, because, like it or not, you are going to work for me."

Kathlyn raised her eyes to heaven in a thank-you. She'd been frantic about not having found a summer job. School was out tomorrow, and her resources had dried up. Whatever he was offering was a godsend.

"And don't go looking up there and asking Him or Her for help. You're the one who suggested that I sell the companies. It's not His fault that it's driving me insane trying to do it. You are going to help me get this under control."

During his tirade David had stalked her, and now she had her back one inch from the statue. His hot-fudge eyes, red-rimmed but still sexy, bored into hers. She smiled. "Okay."

"God, you look fabulous." He lowered his head for a hungry kiss. Her mouth automatically opened for him, and he ran his tongue over the slightly uneven edge of her two front teeth. When his tongue met hers, sparks of electricity shot through her, zinging along nerve endings, and settling in her most private place. "I've missed you, angel. I've missed you so damn much."

His head dipped for another taste, and she savored every drop. He left her lips and nibbled on her neck, working his way up to her ear. "I know I can't have you, baby, but I sure do want you."

Kathlyn was having trouble breathing. His lips were tantalizing, eager, and tasted of delicious, wicked desire. His arms around her made the loneliness of the past weeks disappear. She raised her arms and ran her hands through his thick hair. As if begging her to linger, the curls wrapped around her fingers. She lifted his head with a slight pressure of her hands and claimed his lips for another kiss. This time the kiss was easier, gentler, more loving. This time Kathlyn freely admitted to herself that she was falling in love with him.

"I guess we'd better stop." His breath whispered against the side of her neck.

"Yes." She knew she didn't sound very convincing. Opening his eyes, he looked behind her at the statue, and chuckled. He reached around Kathlyn and patted the ceramic head. "Coffee?" he rasped.

"Coming right up." She eased away from him and headed for the kitchen. Her heart was beating crazily. Falling in love with David? With the man who would never marry? Who only wanted friendship?

Sister Angelica had said that when the right man came along, she would know. And nothing had ever felt this right. Could it mean that David was the man chosen for her, that his reasons for not marrying could be overcome, were not as serious as he thought?

When David returned from the bathroom, his face was damp with water.

"You need a shave," she blurted.

"And a haircut and some sleep." He ran his hand through his hair and across his face. "But what I really need is your promise that you'll help me out. I've already put the financially healthiest businesses on the market, but I have some I'm not sure of. I have to visit each one, take notes, and see what to do with them."

"Where do I come in?" She poured them each a cup of coffee and followed him to her dining table, anxious to hear his answer.

"My secretary quit. She told me she was too old for all my foolishness. I need someone who'll support me."

And, how did you spend your summer, Kathlyn? Jet-setting around and watching a genius at work.

"When do we start?"

"When's your last day of school?"

"Tomorrow."

"The next day, then. Wednesday."

He named a salary figure that left her speechless. He said it so matter-of-factly that she assumed that was the going rate for secretaries. She knew teachers were near the bottom of the pay scale; she just hadn't realized how far down.

"I'll write you a check to cover a couple of months rent and keep the utilities people happy. I don't know how much time you'll spend here. The first stop will be Arizona. There's a cotton mill there we have to see about. Be ready to go Wednesday morning around eight. My driver will pick you up."

Kathlyn smiled as she went to refill his coffee cup. The genius at work was an awesome thing.

When she returned with his coffee, she found him with his head on the table, fast asleep.

She gathered the bedding and made up the couch, then gently shook him awake. She removed his shoes and socks while he took off his suit coat and tie and shirt. He stood groggily to remove his pants, and Kathlyn beat a hasty retreat to the kitchen. When she returned from tidying the room, he was under the covers, sound asleep.

She kissed his rough cheek and smoothed back the curls from his forehead. She straightened and looked over at the statue. "I think I'm going down for the count, Mary." She gave the statue a wink. "Take care of him, okay?"

"You do take shorthand, don't you?"

Kathlyn sat in the cushioned chair, trying not to look like a gawking hick. The plane had a bar and a bedroom, couches and lounge chairs, and a bathroom fit for a shah. There were more luxuries than in her apartment.

"No," she said while trying to get the stupid seat belt fastened. "I'm a music teacher, not a secretary."

David glared at her. She glared right back. He hadn't specified that she needed shorthand.

"Well, you'd better write fast."

"Yes, sir, I'll do my best."

"Smart mouth," David said, but a smile was beginning to play around his tense mouth.

"Dictator." She smiled back at him.

"You just keep that in mind, and we'll get along fine." David came over and snapped her seat belt in place and snapped a hard kiss on her smart mouth at the same time.

The plane took off, and Kathlyn held tightly to the armrests. She'd never flown, and hoped she wouldn't be airsick. After they leveled off, she glanced across the aisle and saw that David was engrossed in studying what looked like volumes of papers. He'd had his hair trimmed. He looked delectable in his black suit, white shirt, and patterned tie. She smiled and began reading the material David had provided about cotton mills.

David concentrated on what he was reading, but even though the facts registered, he knew the minute Kathlyn drifted off to sleep. He set the papers aside and sat looking at her—just looking and enjoying the peace she gave him. After long moments, he again picked up the files and got back to work.

Some hours later the pilot informed him that they were approaching the Tucson area. He stood and stretched.

He knelt down in front of Kathlyn, taking another moment to study her. He found her the loveliest thing he had ever seen. He still believed she could make it as a model. Now, however, he saw so much more. What he felt for her couldn't be love, but it was so much more than he had ever felt for any other woman. He wished it could be love. . . . No, it simply couldn't be.

He leaned over and lightly kissed her baby-soft

cheek. She didn't stir. He shook her gently, whispering, "Time to wake up and start working, Kathlyn."

He watched her eyelids lift to half-mast. She smiled and yawned, quickly covering her mouth with her hand and whispering an apology. David stood up, but couldn't take his eyes off her. She wore her yellow pleated skirt and a short-sleeve white cotton blouse with a feminine bow tied at the neck. Her bare arms and nylon-covered legs were golden tan, a color he assumed was natural, a color he wanted to see on the hidden portions of her body. *Whoa. None of that.*

"Why don't you freshen up before we land? We have about a half an hour's drive from the airport to the mill."

"Thanks." She was trying to remember where she was, trying not to drown in the heated look coming from his eyes.

They arrived at the mill and David was shown, with much scurrying and kowtowing, into an office. Two computers were set up on separate desks, and David expressed his relief that Kathlyn was familiar with the model. She liked computers, and had used a similar one at the business department at school.

They spent the day in the office, breaking only to join the staff for lunch. David would call out a file he needed her to print out, or a bunch of files he wanted her to cross-reference. She flipped through the computer manual efficiently, and much to her surprise, did everything he asked without needing his help. It was six o'clock before he had all the material he needed.

Kathlyn hadn't even thought about their living arrangements. She hadn't cared or worried, knowing David would handle it all. She was a little surprised when he opened only one door on the sixteenth floor of the Tucson hotel and followed her inside. The momentary panic turned to delight when she saw the two-bedroom hotel suite. It was first class, like something she'd read about in novels and seen on glitzy TV shows. If she hadn't been so exhausted, she would have reveled in the luxury.

David pointed her to one door and headed for the one across the blue-carpeted living area. "Change into something comfortable. I'll call down for room service."

Kathlyn showered and put on her flowing caftan. When she returned to the living area, he was behind the light wood-grained bar pouring her a glass of wine. His hair was damp from his shower, and his shirt was half-buttoned. When he came from behind the bar, she noticed that his feet were bare, like hers. She laughed and wiggled her toes in the lush carpeting. "Feels good, hey?"

"It feels terrific."

Their meal was delivered before they could take the first sips of their drinks. Instead of sitting at the round glass table inside the suite, they opted for the wrought-iron table on the patio. The view of the mountains and the desert was enthralling, but their main focus right then was food. There were covered dishes of steak and potatoes and vegetables. A solid meal, a meal needed to recoup their strength.

"That was great." Kathlyn sat back and sipped her drink, absorbing the magnificent sight of the fireball sun setting behind the majestic mountains.

"Not bad." David relaxed with his own drink. "Boring day, wasn't it?"

"Heavens, no. It was very challenging for me."

David slouched down a little in his chair, and Kathlyn could see the tension he'd built up during the tedious day easing out of him.

"Tomorrow will be different," he said. "Wear your jeans and sneakers and an old top. We're going to join the work force and see the nitty-gritty of making raw cotton into fabric."

Kathlyn's eyes lit up. A soul mate, he thought. Someone who understood his need to know and to see how things were produced.

During the next two days, Kathlyn saw blending machines, cleaning machines, and picking machines which knocked dirt out of the cotton. She watched the carding machine separate and straighten the cotton fibers, and the combers strengthen the fibers and make them more lustrous. The spinning process held her spellbound until David interrupted, demanding the files on the efficiency of the machines, of the department as a whole. She scribbled notes as fast as she could in a shorthand only she could read.

Each night when they arrived back at the suite, Kathlyn showered and translated her notes for David. Late Friday night he studied the last of the notes and shook his head.

"There doesn't seem to be a way for this mill to compete with the larger textile mills in the Southeast. All we work with here is cotton. The purpose for starting the mill was that the cotton could be milled closer to its source of growth and baling. But it isn't working out financially. Everything's on the up and up, and they're producing as efficiently as they can, but the cost of their products is higher than the mills in, say, North Carolina.

"I have no choice but to admit defeat on this one. Damn, I was really hoping it could be saved." He rose tiredly to his feet. "You worked like a Trojan. Thanks, honey."

Kathlyn fell asleep remembering the "honey," worrying about how hard David worked, and thinking what a shame it was to close down the mill.

In the middle of the night she sat straight up in bed. She and David were concerned about the fact that so many Native Americans were about to become unemployed. How about . . . ? What if . . . ?

"David," she cried as she struggled into her caftan. With the garment covering her eyes, she ran smack into him as he rushed out of his room.

"Oof." He grabbed her before she fell.

"Ouch." She rubbed her nose where it had collided with his chest.

"I think I've got it," they said at the same time.

"You do?" They echoed again, and started laughing.

They looked at each other speculatively. "Native Americans?" Kathlyn whispered tentatively.

"Right! Get me the phone book."

He plowed through the yellow pages and came up with what he was looking for. "I thought I heard one of the workers say that his wife worked at a garment factory owned by the tribe. Look. It's close to the mill. Suppose, now, just suppose, that the tribal leaders wanted to buy the mill? Suppose they use their own designer to design the patterns for the material instead of using the same prints that the other mills are using? They could design cloth original to them and then take it to the garment factory to be made into sheets or dresses or whatever. What do you think, angel? Was that what you had in mind?"

"Yes." Kathlyn couldn't believe they had both come up with the same idea at the same time.

David whooped and rushed over to lift her up and swing her around in a circle. "Dress up pretty tomorrow, angel, and take good notes. We'll need them to draw up the contract if the council goes for it."

* * *

What was there not to go for? Kathlyn silently asked herself as she sat before the council in her taupe, jewel-neck blouse and darker front-pleated, straight skirt. David was offering them the company for the price of the building and the machinery. If the plans did not materialize for the mill, all they had to do was sell the machinery and building and come out even. And this, she gathered from the look David gave her as he told her what to write down, was what his last secretary had objected to. Where was the profit? Where was the hard-bargaining businessman? Not here. David's big thrill, his challenge, was in making a company profitable, not how much he could make doing it.

That night he took Kathlyn out to dinner. The restaurant was plush and upbeat. The food was excellent, the delicious dessert wicked, the music sensual, and his companion slightly tipsy.

"I think you're the sexiest man I know," she whispered on the way back to the hotel. Her head, resting against the seat back, was turned toward him.

"And how many do you know?"

"Well, I've seen plenty. A group of us went to one of those male strip shows. There wasn't one of them who had a chest sexier than yours."

Lord, she was going to kill herself in the morning. He was trying very hard to hold in laughter as he tried to picture Kathlyn at the strip show. "Did you blush a lot, angel?"

"At the strip show, or at seeing your chest?" she asked seriously.

David's cheek was getting numb from biting it. "Both."

"I don't think I blushed when I saw your chest. It really is very well put together. I didn't blush at the strip joint, either, except when I tucked that dollar bill into the man's, uh, you know.''

David bit down harder.

"Anyway, their bodies were all smooth, like they had shaved off all the hair on their chest and legs. They still had some under their arms. That was kind of sexy.''

"Kathlyn, quit. You're going to make me have an accident.''

"There's a rest room up ahead.''

He couldn't hold it in any longer. His laugh broke out, but he tried to hide it with a cough. "Not that kind of an accident. And what inspired you to go to one of those shows?''

"Once I had accepted that I was going to get married, I thought I'd better do some research. I read a lot of magazines that explain how a woman and a man act on dates, or what it is that a man is thinking when he says stuff like you said to me about going to bed.''

"Good Lord, what else would he be thinking?''

"Well, the obvious, of course. But they explained how, deep down, some men don't really mean that. They try that approach because they think women want to hear it.''

"I think that's a bunch of bull!''

"Hmmm. Maybe you should write an article for them.''

"I doubt they'd print it. Go on.''

"I decided after all that reading that it wouldn't do any harm to see a male body, in the flesh, so to speak.''

"Why, for heaven's sake?''

"I'm going to go into marriage pure, David, but I don't want to be ignorant, or completely surprised, on my wedding night.''

"Seeing your husband's chest won't make you faint?"

"Right. I can enjoy looking at it rather than blushing."

"And when the pants come off? That won't bother you, either?"

"No, I've seen male legs."

"I meant when the shorts come off."

She laughed deep in her throat. "Some things are better left as surprises, don't you think? Anyway, I've read medical journals, and know what to expect."

David sat behind the wheel shaking his head. Her next words shocked him completely.

"Are they all pretty much alike?"

He swallowed back the bark of laughter and couldn't answer her.

"I wish I had a mother I could ask. Sister Angelica is an understanding soul, but I doubt she'd be able to answer my questions."

"Probably not," David said, gulping. "Well, I think they're pretty much the same, more or less."

Kathlyn burst out laughing.

David felt himself redden. "I didn't mean that. I meant that they all operate in the same manner."

"Yes, I know. I've seen pictures, sort of before and after."

As David pulled into the hotel's parking lot, Kathlyn looked troubled. "What's bothering you now?"

"I was wondering if it always hurts the first time."

"I don't think so, angel. Not if the man cares enough to get you ready."

"Have you ever done it with a virgin?"

"No."

"I think you'd make the woman ready, wouldn't you?"

"Always."

He had to get out of the car before he showed her how ready she could get. As he was reaching for the door handle, she stopped him with another worry. "What if I have one of those hymens that can't be broken?"

David sighed deeply. "Kathlyn, stop worrying. Before you get married, ask your doctor. He'll reassure you."

"I hope so. Is making love as embarrassing as having a pelvic exam?"

He turned back to her and cupped her sweet, worried face in his hands. "No, darling, making love is absolutely the most beautiful act a man and a woman can do together."

She sighed before she closed the short distance between them and pecked him on the lips. "Yes. I figured God had to make it that way, or there wouldn't be many babies, would there?"

Babies? He quickly got out of the car and came around to open her door. "Can you make it up to the suite?"

"Yes. I'm fine. Just lead me in the right direction."

Just lead me in the right direction. And what direction was that? Away from him?

David walked Kathlyn to the door of her bedroom. It was an enormous effort to control his wish to take her all the way to her bed. She seemed steady enough, just weary. Because he couldn't deny himself a small part of her, he bent and kissed her softly on the lips. Kathlyn wrapped her arms around his neck and drew him into a deep kiss. She sighed against his lips and opened her mouth.

David lost control. He opened his mouth to her questing tongue. His arms tightened around her waist and drew her snugly against him. His arousal had begun with their conversation in the car. Her sweet licking and sighing and moaning painfully completed it. God, she was so delicious. More so than any woman he'd ever known.

Damn! This was Kathlyn Marie McDaniel, almost-nun, marriage-minded.

Slowly, reluctantly, he went about breaking the kiss. He ran his tongue over her lips, tasting her, tasting himself. He placed two sweet, gentle kisses on her lips and slowly opened his eyes to look at her. Good God! She was ready to be made love to. Her eyelids were shut, and her mouth was searching for his. Her hands at the back of his neck were slack. Her head fell forward to rest on his chest while her breath whispered unevenly from between puffy lips.

He caressed her back, trying to bring her down from the sexual high. He didn't know what would do that for him, but he'd figure that out after he got away from her.

He reached behind her, opened her door, and said, "Go to bed, angel."

She lifted her eyelids, her blue eyes glazed, and David almost dragged her back to him.

"Good night, David. Thanks for the dinner, for the whole day." She reached up and kissed him one more time and entered her room, closing the door behind her.

"Good night, David," he mimicked as he stormed toward his room. Hell! Didn't she have a clue as to what her kisses and her body did to him? Surely in all that reading she claimed to have done, somebody must have mentioned arousing the male. He headed straight for the shower, cursing naive women. The water was freezing, but David stood braced beneath it, with his hands against the sides of the shower. His head was down, and the water streamed over his body. Having her with him the entire summer was probably a mistake. But, damn it, he liked having her near. The past days had been tiring, as usual, but more exhilarating than ever before.

What a mess!

She was under him. Reaching out with silken golden arms to embrace him. Her body beckoned. The heat rose between them. Her gorgeous full breasts heaved with the desire he had aroused in her. She was glistening with perspiration. So was he. Never had he felt this urgency about possessing a woman. Kathlyn. God, Kathlyn! He began to penetrate, going slowly, trying not to hurt her. Her soft lips were on his neck, her low, sexy voice begging him to come into her. He wasn't sure he could penetrate the barrier she'd saved just for him without exploding first. He pressed forward with extreme care. He kissed her. He teased her breasts with the hair on his chest, and he moved forward.

She screamed! She twisted her head and her body trying to get away from him. He tried to gentle her while still going forward into her virgin body. She screamed again, and cried out. He couldn't get through. Her hymen was not penetrable! What now? He couldn't retreat. He couldn't go forward. He was ready to explode! He screamed out in frustration. And woke himself.

He turned onto his back and sprang to a sitting position, doubling over in pain. His body was soaked with sweat, making him shiver in the air conditioning even though his body burned as if he were in the depths of hell. He rocked back and forth, taking in deep breaths. Finally, after what seemed like hours, he slowly lay back on the bed, grimacing at the pain in his wracked body. He pulled the sheet up to his neck, trying to get warm, and inhaled deeply one more time. His heart was slowing to normal; his battered manhood still ached, but decreased in size.

Not once had he been this uncontrollably aroused. By a virgin, an ex-nun who could never be anything more than his friend.

He stretched and put one hand under his head on the pillow. As far as he could see, he had two choices. One: Take her back to Atlanta, pay her for the summer, and not see her again. No. He'd never had a friend like her—one who was willing to go to the ends of the earth with him. Two: Continue as they were, with her working alongside of him, and him trying to keep his emotions under control. Possible, but not easy.

He turned onto his side, snuggling the spare pillow to his chest. He yawned and closed his gritty eyes. *You have one other choice*, something in his subconscious whispered temptingly. *You could sleep with her every night, wake with her every morning. Come home to her every night.*

Kathlyn. Home. Marriage.

David awoke the next morning sore from his embarrassing battle with the sheet. He rolled over, stretched, and wished Kathlyn were beside him. *Wake with her. Marriage.* His heart picked up a crazy tattoo. Excitement? No, fear. In the light of day he remembered the futility of wishful thinking.

But he still had her as his friend. He recalled their conversation in the car last night and grinned. She was really going to be embarrassed. David imagined her rosy cheeks as he teased her about some of her questions. Well, maybe he wouldn't. She had said she had no one else to talk to. He found that he didn't mind being the one. However, he couldn't help anticipating her chagrined expression.

As he came out of his bedroom, Kathlyn and the waiter bearing breakfast entered the outer door of the suite.

"Where've you been?"

"You were still sleeping, so I went to early Mass. And good morning to you, too." She came up to him and kissed him on the cheek.

"Uh, good morning," he answered. His gaze followed her as she walked to the table on the terrace. She looked fresh and smart in a short, white, straight skirt and matching long-sleeve, fitted jacket. The skirt hugged her rounded bottom like a dream, and the slit at the back of the hem added a certain tease when it exposed more of her golden legs.

He glanced at the waiter. The boy was nearly salivating as he, too, watched Kathlyn. David felt like ramming his fist into the boy's open mouth. Instead he shoved some bills into the kid's hand and gave him a gentle push toward the door. After all, such a natural male reaction wasn't the kid's fault.

"Thanks for ordering." Kathlyn gave a self-deprecating laugh. "I'm starving, as usual."

David seated himself and looked at the woman across from him. Sensual, alluring, innocent. And most definitely not chagrined. Surely she hadn't forgotten their conversation in the car? Surely she hadn't forgotten their explosive kisses?

She buttered herself a piece of toast. "Oh, by the way, thanks for answering my questions last night. I know you were probably uncomfortable, but if I don't get answers, I worry myself silly."

David shook his head. The woman drove him crazy. "You're welcome." He thought this was a good time to lecture her. "However, you must understand that some men would have reacted quite differently from the way I did."

"Oh? How?"

"Well, the conversation we had might have turned some men on. Our kiss might have encouraged them to take advantage. I just thought you might like to know, so you can be careful." *Huh! You can't stand the thought of her asking any other man personal questions. You're jealous just thinking about her kissing another man.*

And look at her listening to you as if you were the teacher and she the student—as if your advice was coming from a . . . friend.

She nodded her head. "Thanks. I'll keep that in mind."

He frowned as he wondered if his jealousy was the reason he had insisted that Kathlyn spend the summer with him. He knew she was looking for a husband. Was he afraid she would find one in his absence? And if he was trying to prevent that, what right did he have? *Unless . . .* There went his subconscious again. *Unless you marry her.*

A trickle of fear ran down his spine. His hands began to shake as he tried to lift his fork to his mouth. He knew better than to think about marriage. All he had to do was picture his mother. *But you're not your mother.*

The portable fax machine began to spurt out a message. Relieved, he went over to it. With hands still unsteady, he pulled the sheet from the machine and read it.

Kathlyn had sat watching David. His face had clouded up, his mind working out a problem. He got so intense when trying to figure something out. She knew better than to try to say anything. So she had simply looked at him, enjoying the view of the man she loved. Oh, yes. She had finally admitted it the night before, lying awake for long moments reliving their kiss and his caresses, respecting him for not pushing her into the bedroom and into an affair she couldn't live with.

She had lain there and tried out the logic she had learned in college. A: She knew God had called her to the married life. B: After almost two years of searching, she had fallen in love with David. He desired her. She desired him. He cared about her. She cared about him. He wanted to be friends, but friends didn't kiss the way he had kissed her last night. And with that kiss she had committed herself to him. He was . . . well, not committed, yet. But since A was true and so was all of B, her conclusion was simple. C: She and David St. John were going to get married. He was *the* one.

She raised her eyes to heaven and prayed for the patience to wait for David to realize that he loved her and had nothing to fear from marriage.

David turned to Kathlyn in time to see her looking heavenward. He rolled his eyes. The woman definitely needed more earthly friends to communicate with.

"My lawyer thinks I'm a fool for the mill deal, but says everything is legally ready for the signing. He also reminded me that I had promised to talk to a friend in Galveston, Texas. Since we're so close, I'll see if I can't line up a meeting with him this afternoon. I won't need you on this one, angel. You can spend the day sunning."

No, he wouldn't need her on this one. In fact, he didn't want her along for the meeting. The friend was trying to get him to invest in a low-income housing project. David didn't want Kathlyn along when he turned down a plan to help the poor. In all reality, it would probably help only the developer. Little Miss Goody Two-Shoes had better stay home on this deal.

SEVEN

Kathlyn Marie McDaniel, you are a menace!

David headed back to the Galveston hotel driving a compact rental car. Even though he had not taken Kathlyn to the meeting, she had been there in spirit. His friend had shown such enthusiasm and dedication about the low-income housing project that David had gotten caught up in it. All the while he'd been reading and signing the papers endorsing the project, he'd had a vision of Kathlyn's delighted face. Odd, but he had also felt something else—as if someone *up there* had been pleased with his decision.

Hell. All these years he'd been minding his own business, doing what he had to do without drawing the attention of the *higher—ups*. Kathlyn had probably sicced *them* on him.

Back at the hotel, David picked up Kathlyn's note and walked to the window overlooking the Gulf of Mexico. He read the note again and smiled. She'd be the one in the orange bathing suit. Kind of hard to miss, even across the wide expanse of white beach. He frowned. She was playing volleyball with a bunch of beach jocks. And, damn it, that suit was fluorescent orange, one piece and skimpy!

He watched her playing hard, smacking the ball. He watched the men watching Kathlyn bounce and roll. When one of the men "accidentally" knocked her to the sand, David rushed into his room and snatched on his bathing suit so quickly, it was a wonder he didn't hurt something.

By the time he got down to the beach, Kathlyn was heading into the rolling, blue surf, her movements graceful and strong. She was floating on her back when he came up alongside of her.

"Hi." He rolled onto his back and floated next to her while the warm water undulated beneath his body.

She turned her head and gave him a smile. "Hi, yourself. Did the meeting go well?"

"Yeah." His eyes devoured the outline of her breasts under the wet, clinging suit. Her nipples were hidden by the suit's bra, but his imagination was getting better and better each time he saw her. His gaze skimmed down the orange, finding the delightful expanse of skin. The suit was cut on the side nearly to her hips, the skin evenly golden. Her legs, long and sleek and gorgeous, floated on the water.

He reached out for her hand and linked his with hers. The contact was both arousing and reassuring. The longer they floated together on this natural water bed, the more aroused David became. The hair on his chest stood up, and the part that proclaimed him male rose beneath his black trunks.

He turned, wanting to take her in his arms and kiss her. She made a move toward him as if she wanted it, too. A whopping wave broke violently over their heads. They sank, then came up for air, hands still joined like lifelines. They sputtered and coughed and laughed just as another wave broke, knocking them once again beneath the water. When their feet could touch bottom, they water-ran toward the shore.

"I forgot to watch how far we drifted in," Kathlyn gasped, still choking, still laughing, still feeling the overpowering urge to kiss him. She wanted to lick the water from his hairy chest like a thirsty cat, to kiss his salt-watered lips, to run her hands over every sleek inch of him. Loving him had turned the yearning into compulsion. She took in shallow breaths as she watched him dry himself off.

She spread her towel on the sand and, not wanting him to see the pointy rise of her nipples, fell facedown on the towel. Her breasts made contact with the hard sand, and she bit her tongue to keep from groaning. Laying her head on her arms, she fought to bring herself under control. It was working until he spoke and his sweet breath tickled over her like the warm Gulf breeze.

She lifted her head and stared into his eyes. The rest of the world disappeared. Facing her, he rested his chin on his hands, their bodies at a 180-degree angle. She cupped her chin in her hands, her elbows planted in the sand. David looked down at the neckline of her suit. It only gaped slightly. Damn, the suit fit too tightly across her bosom to suit him. The slight line of cleavage made him hungry for more, especially as he watched a stray, lucky drop of water slide into the valley between her breasts.

He looked up into her smoky blue eyes. He fought for air. He leaned closer. She leaned closer. Their lips met. Once, lightly. Twice, lingeringly. The third time, open and hungry. Tongues entwined while their hands stayed firmly anchored under their chins. The surf quieted. The sea gulls disappeared. The only sounds were their own sweet sighs and throaty moans.

"I, uh, take it this means you don't care to play volleyball?"

Kathlyn broke from David's lips with a jerk. They looked up to see a well-built sun goddess covered only by three skimpy pieces of chartreuse material. Kathlyn's eyes narrowed. "You take that right!"

The girl shrugged and walked away, showing off her rear end in the thong bathing suit. Kathlyn's mouth dropped open, and David laughed. Kathlyn glared at him, which only made him laugh harder.

"Unless you want a face full of sand, David St. John, I suggest you stop."

"Yes, ma'am." He leaned over and kissed her swiftly.

She grunted.

There should have been something wrong with Kathlyn's jealousy, David thought. It wasn't supposed to make him want to beat his chest or crow like a rooster. Oh, what the hell. That was exactly how he did feel, so why worry about it? Why couldn't he simply enjoy whatever feelings she brought his way?

They both rested for a while, enjoying the salty air, the Gulf breeze, and the sun soaking into every muscle like a delicious elixir.

Kathlyn broke the silence, again planting her elbows in the sand and resting her chin in the palms of her hands. "There's a little boy at school whose parents are not at all supportive of his above-average intelligence. How did your parents act? Were they proud of you?"

David mimicked her posture and smiled. "Yes, they were. Mom was a kick. We played games and solved puzzles all the time. She used to go out to rummage sales and pick up broken appliances, or lamps, or anything that could be taken apart and put back together. She'd bring the stuff home and deposit it in the room she had turned into a workshop for me. I was only six or seven. It fascinated me to see how things were put together, how they worked. I guess I was the only kid who could build an appliance but not plug it in.''

"She wasn't that confident in your ability, huh?''

"Not after the first time she plugged in the mixer I had fixed. We had to use the fire extinguisher.'' His smile lingered, but some of the happiness dimmed in his eyes. "God, she was a joy. In fact, she laughed so hard after the fire was out, she could barely tell my dad what had happened.''

"And your dad?''

"He was a banker. He came to all of my baseball games, even though I was only the water boy.''

"Water boy?'' Kathlyn was indignant. "No one in Little League is a water boy. They all have to be allowed to play.''

"Right. Well, I kind of had a habit of stopping the game, losing it for my team by staring at the ball—wondering how it was made, or calculating the distance between the bases to see if they had been set up properly.''

Kathlyn was shaking her head. "David, David.''

"My father wound up taking the whole bunch of us to a sporting goods factory to see how the equipment was made. He took us to an ice cream factory, a bubble gum factory, and all sorts of places of discovery. The kids didn't want to be cut out of any of that, so they asked me if I would take over the very vital position of water boy. I mean, the whole team could have died of thirst if I hadn't done my job. Right?''

"Right.'' Kathlyn leaned forward and kissed him.

"And you let them all believe you had swallowed their line."

David shrugged. "I got to be a little boy for a while. To wear the team uniform. I loved it."

And I love you, she thought, feeling the emotion grow in her with every new thing she learned about him.

"Are your parents still alive?"

"Dad was diagnosed with cancer when I was sixteen. He died two years later. Mom's in a private nursing home in Atlanta."

Kathlyn could see the pain in his eyes. Pain because of the loss of his father, but more so when he spoke of his mother. Before Kathlyn could decide about the wisdom of probing further, he was speaking again.

"I still have my grandpap, though. He lives on the old homestead south of Atlanta. He's an ornery old coot who'll probably live to be a hundred."

Now his eyes revealed the joy he felt in loving the old man. She also saw that devil's twinkle of his, and was shocked to realize how long it had been since it had last appeared. "You take after him, I presume?"

"I'm not ornery."

Kathlyn laughed.

"I'll get you for that, Kathlyn Marie McDaniel."

He started to rise, but Kathlyn was up and running. He didn't catch her until they were waist-deep in the water, and he didn't dunk her, as she had expected. He caught her up in his arms and kissed her while they sank below the surf. She became lost in the quiet blue depths of the water and the depth of the kiss. Her arms tightened around his shoulders; her mouth devoured his tongue.

Their bodies floated to the surface until they were once again in the sunlight, still locked in the kiss and each other's arms. He dug his feet into the sandy bottom as a brace against the waves and hugged her tighter. She ran her hands along his muscled arms, shoulders, and back and finally up into his rich, curly hair. She held his head to keep his lips on hers. His hand covered her breast, and Kathlyn had to break the kiss in order to draw in air. He cupped her breast and rubbed his thumb across the nipple. It immediately sprang to life, hardened, begged for more. She laid her head against the side of his neck, trying to breathe while the feelings of urgency and arousal sailed through her body. It felt so right to have him touch her as no man ever had. It *was* right! She breathed deeply again, smelling salt water and David. Her entire body was surrounded by and absorbed into him. He was hers. Hers!

"Enough, angel. God, but you pack a wallop."

"Me?" She hadn't done a thing. It was he who packed the punch.

"I think," David said, trying to sound as if he were breathing normally, "that we'd better take a final swim and then head up to the hotel. I'd like to get back to Atlanta this evening." No way could he spend the night with her in the adjoining room.

"You mean we booked the hotel just for the afternoon?"

Kathlyn leaned forward and pushed him hard. Caught off balance, David flailed his arms and fell backwards into the surf. She swam as if she were on the last leg of a marathon. When he caught up with her, he grabbed her and kissed her again as they went under. He was, in more ways than one, in way over his head!

On the plane ride home, Kathlyn read one of the magazines she had purchased at the airport. She needed to think about something besides David St. John, her reaction to him, his reaction to her, and where those reactions could take them. She knew he wasn't ready *yet*, for the final commitment, that he believed he would never marry. She couldn't figure out why. They would be good together, and soon, she prayed, he'd realize it, too.

After finishing the article, she settled the magazine on her lap and sighed.

"What was the sigh for?"

She leaned against the plush seat back and turned her head toward him, reluctant to answer. Then she said softly, "The article I just read was . . . about grand passions, bondings between two people so deep, so lasting, so special sexually, that they come only once in a lifetime, if one is lucky enough to meet the right person. Loves that last forever."

"Kathlyn, you can't believe everything you read."

She sighed again. "I know. But wouldn't it be wonderful to meet the right one, and share that special devotion to each other? Wouldn't it be marvelous to live the rest of your life with your grand passion?

"Another article claimed that there were forty thousand people with whom each person could live happily and comfortably. I would rather have the grand passion."

"Maybe such a strong passion isn't comfortable," David said. He felt that his obsession with Kathlyn could almost be classified as a grand passion. He didn't find that at all comfortable.

Kathlyn shrugged her shoulders. "Many of the couples in this article went from that great partner to marry others. Some of them still thought about that one great love off and on. Some went in search of that first partner, even abandoning their families. Why are people so dumb that they can't recognize true love in the beginning?''

"Kathlyn, angel. I think you're getting wrapped up in a fairy tale. Lovely and romantic, but a fantasy. In real life, people have jobs. They argue. They have responsibilities to their children, their spouses.''

His voice hardened. "And through all the hardships and personal crises, they're supposed to keep loving each other and trying to make each other happy. Life, my dear, is not one great big orgasm of grand passion.''

Kathlyn winced at his sharp tone. She'd hit a nerve, an exposed one. She wanted to soothe and heal it if she could. "Want to talk about it?''

"What?''

Not yet, she thought. But someday he'd talk. Someday he'd admit the ache was there.

"Never mind.'' She turned her head forward and picked up the magazine. "But thanks for shooting a hole in my romantic bubble.''

God, he felt as if he'd kicked a three-legged dog. But, damn it, she just couldn't go around expecting married life to resemble romantic fiction. What was romantic about watching a woman shave under her arms? About starting your day with a disheveled wife yawning at you from across the breakfast table? About hearing your partner snore through the night? And what the hell was romantic about two people completely destroying each other for the sake of marriage?

He opened his mouth to say all that, but out came, "I'm sorry.''

She gave a brisk wave. "No. You're probably right. If a marriage was based only on grand sexual passion, it wouldn't survive. One night she'd be ready for a mind-boggling sexual encounter, and he'd be sick in the bathroom.''

You'd warm him when he was chilled, wouldn't you, angel? You'd bathe his brow and body with cool water when he had a fever, and you'd wear something sexy and alluring while doing it to show him what he had to look forward to when he got better. David sighed longingly.

Kathlyn sighed too, forlornly. Did she have to wait years for him to decide he loved her? To decide to trust her enough to reveal his inner thoughts and feelings? Years? She sighed again, despairingly.

When Kathlyn entered David's posh office on Monday, he smiled and said, "Morning." He bent and kissed her softly, and her heart did a magnificent swan dive. He looked so wonderful. So businesslike. So sumptuous in his dark gray suit and white pristine shirt. His tie was a little askew, so Kathlyn reached up and adjusted it, patting it when she was done.

"Thanks," David said, feeling a sense of mild panic at the wifely gesture.

"So where do you want me?"

In bed, damn it! Shame on you, David. This is a workplace, where the grand passion turns to reality. The place where you are going to titillate Kathlyn's curiosity and challenge her skills. He could hardly wait to begin.

"As you've noticed, I hired a new in-office secretary. You'll still travel with me, but while I handle the sale of some of the businesses, I have a special project for you."

They descended to the basement. It looked just like another floor of offices, well lit and clean. David took a key from his pocket, opened a set of double doors, and flipped on the lights.

Kathlyn gasped as she looked around. The huge room contained at least a hundred shelves completely stocked with boxes of many sizes and shapes. Each shelf contained six levels. Along the floor sat boxes and boxes of oversize items.

"What I want you to do, Kathlyn, is get rid of this stuff for me." He walked to a desk and took a stack of papers from the top drawer. "Here's a partial list of the inventory. The stock is left from a mail-order novelty business that went under. The items range from the practical to the absurd, from the serious to the ridiculous. I don't care where or how you sell them or if you give some of them away, but I need to make this amount on the sales." He circled a figure on the bottom of the last page. It looked like an outrageous amount to her.

"You're kidding, right?"

"No, that's what I want to get out of the stock."

"No. What I meant was, you're kidding about having me do this. What do I know about selling such a large quantity?"

"You don't have to know anything. You only have to figure out what you're going to sell for how much. Then I'll have one of the secretaries help you locate where you can try to unload them. Simple."

Simple. Simple-minded, that's what he was!

David watched as her doubt was replaced with the sparkle he'd seen in her eyes when they'd been in Tucson. Oh, yes, she was going to take up the challenge. He knew she had it in her to see it through successfully. He knew he was falling in love with her. *Steady, David.*

"Questions?"

"Probably a million that I can't think of right now."

"If you need any help, just call. The numbers are on the desk." He hugged her briefly. "Don't worry about rushing it, as long as it's done by the end of the summer.'' He turned and left her before he could give in to his desire to throw her down on the boxes and make love to her.

By the end of the summer? Two and a half months before she had to start teaching again. There was no way she'd have this done by then. Well, she'd certainly give it her best shot!

By the end of the day, her dress was white where it had been navy, and gray where it had been white. Her feet felt tortured. She dragged herself onto the subway and gratefully found a seat. The transit car rumbled smoothly along, and she fell asleep, nearly missing her stop. She had to take off her heels and walk the two short blocks to her apartment. The few stones she stepped on were no worse than the torture of her pointed shoes.

She laughed as she unlocked her door. David had been right. Some of the items she was cataloging were ridiculous. *And, what did you do today, Kathlyn? I read dumb jokes on toilet paper*. She could hardly wait to see what was in the rest of the boxes.

She picked up the ringing phone, still chuckling.

"How'd it go?'' His voice was magnificent. "The job isn't too difficult, is it?''

"No. It's going to be fine. By the way, I'm wearing jeans and running shoes tomorrow. Objection?''

"Only a personal one. Your legs are too magnificent to cover. Your rear does look great in jeans, though. I guess one will compensate for the other.''

This from the man who said that romance disappeared when a couple went to work?

David berated himself. It wasn't fair to keep leading her on this way. But then, he was the one in a constant state of arousal. If he married her . . .

"David? Are you still there?''

"Sorry, just wrestling with an impossible problem."

"Nothing's impossible for you, David."

Want to bet? "Listen, I'll let you get cleaned up and get something cooking. I'll be over in an hour."

"You'll what?"

"You will feed me, won't you?" As an actor, he was pitiful.

"Cut it out, David. Your vocation is not the stage. However, there is one leaving in five minutes if you want to get on it."

"Groan. That was bad, angel."

Kathlyn laughed. She figured she was half-punchy from climbing up and down the ladder at work, but completely punchy from the prospect of David sharing her dinner. "Come on over when you're ready. I have some spaghetti sauce in the freezer. See you in a little while."

She took out the sauce and set it in a pot on the stove to simmer. She scrubbed off all the dust and sweat under the shower and took the time to blow-dry her hair, leaving it down and flowing around her face and shoulders. She was just going to stir the sauce again when the doorbell rang.

"You're earl— Oh, hi, Phil. Come on in. Where's Sandra?"

"The girls had a shower for her tonight, so I thought I'd drop by and see what you were doing. Hey, that smells good. Mind if I join you?"

"No. There's plenty. Have a seat and keep me company while I get the rest of it together."

"Been worried about you. I tried to call all last week and didn't get an answer. Did you find a job?"

"Phil, you wouldn't believe the job I'm doing. I'm working as David St. John's secretary while he inspects some of his companies. Last week we were in Tucson and Galveston. This week, while he's taking care of some business at the office, I'm in charge of selling a warehouse full of novelty items. Sure beats working at the grocery store.''

"You're working with David? Traveling around the country with him? Kathlyn, do you think that's safe or wise?''

"Stop fussing. David knows how I feel about premarital sex. He respects my conviction. And I can't tell you how exciting it is to watch him in action.''

"The action better not be in the bedroom,'' Phil said darkly.

"I said stop, Phil. I'm a big girl. I can handle myself. Anyway, David and I are friends.'' Yes, they were. But, oh, how much deeper that friendship was going.

"Okay. I'm sorry, kid. Guess it's kind of become a habit watching over you.''

"Thanks. I appreciate it, but it's not necessary. Oh, my gosh. I completely forgot about our performance next week. I have no idea if I'll be in town. In fact, the entire summer is going to be questionable. If you don't mind, I'll call Janet to fill in.''

"It's all right with me, but I'll miss you. You have a certain knack with that cello that makes it weep or dance with joy. You have talent.''

"Thanks. I'll miss not being able to perform.''

As they talked, she'd tossed together a salad. Water was beginning to steam on the stove, and the delicious aroma of garlic and parmesan cheese from the rolls browning in the oven filled the air. She handed Phil three place mats and plates and asked him to set the table.

"Three?''

"Yes. David is joining us.''

"He'll be thrilled to see me," Phil said, smiling wryly.

"You're his friend. Why wouldn't he be?"

"Come on, Kathlyn, you're not that dense."

The doorbell rang and Kathlyn turned away, hiding her blush. She'd like nothing better than to proclaim loudly that she and David were an item.

"Hi." David walked into the room and kissed her. He spotted Phil and shook hands with him. "I gather you're joining us."

"Yup. Got kicked out of the house while the girls surprised Sandra with a bridal shower. You don't mind, do you?"

"Sandra?"

"My fiancée."

David was shocked at the relief he felt, and . . . envy? "Congratulations, buddy. Glad you could join us tonight. This will give us a chance to renew our friendship."

David couldn't remember the last time he had eaten in such a casual setting. Other women had cooked for him, but the table had always been set with candles, and the entire meal had been foreplay for what was to come. This was simply a relaxed gathering.

After dinner Kathlyn regaled them with novelty toilet tissue jokes. David laughed at Kathlyn's delivery of those outrageous punch lines rather than at the jokes themselves.

Before leaving, David and Phil set Sunday for a barbecue and get-together with their college buddies. After Phil got married, David would be the only single one left. He immediately invited Kathlyn to the barbecue. Damned if he'd face all that domestic bliss without her in tow.

At work the next day, David signed away the first

of the businesses he'd put on the market. Weeks earlier the bids had come flooding in at ridiculously low prices. David had immediately let it be known that he was not filing for Chapter Eleven, merely getting out of his present venture. The field had narrowed to sincere bidders, and negotiations were now a daily thing.

He sat at his desk, hands linked behind his head, a grin creasing his face, pleased with the deal he had just closed on the paper mill. He had gotten fair market value, but more important, a written guarantee on job security for the employees.

The ball was rolling, each turn bringing him closer to a new beginning. He reached for the phone and made dinner reservations. He felt like celebrating!

Kathlyn was in the basement sorting out a box of Halloween costumes. They must have hung on a display somewhere and then been shoved into this box, coat hangers and all. She hummed along with the music on a local radio station as she took the outfits out and hung them along one of the steel shelves. So far that morning she had inventoried masks, face paint, fake vomit, rubber eyeballs, and assorted witches, pumpkins, and skulls. She was a little queasy and slaphappy.

She pulled out a bright purple imitation feather boa from the bottom of the box and absently draped it around her neck. Smiling, she took a skull and placed it on the shelf above the hanging skeleton costume. Witches' faces went above Batman and ballerina outfits. Pumpkin heads completed a ghost and a pirate. To her own dusty jeans, white T-shirt and boa ensemble she added rubber monster hands.

"The Stripper" was blasting from the radio. Grabbing hold of the purple boa with the ghoulish digits, she started to sway. A few tentative jerks of her body turned into a series of bumps and grinds.

Not bad, she thought, and bumped, ground, shimmied, and teased her odd audience. The boa snapped, trailed, and curled around her body as she moved up and down the aisle. Her frenzied movements built to a climax right along with the music. She was panting, laughing, and sweating when the song was finished.

As she took a bow, two powerful hands grabbed her shoulders. She screamed and whirled on her attacker, hitting out with rubber claws!

"Damn it! It's me!" David had to shout above the blaring music of a commercial while fending off her attack. He caught the next scream and pieces of the boa in his mouth as it clamped over hers. He lifted his head and spat out the strands of plastic.

Kathlyn sagged with relief against his body. His arms were bands of steel around her. His heart was beating as fast as hers, but not from fright, she guessed. She could feel the iron length of his manhood pressed against her abdomen.

David knew that if he lived to be a hundred, he'd never forget the dance he'd just witnessed. He groaned and opened his eyes. An almost nun!

He grabbed her shoulders and jerked her away from his body. "What the hell is the matter with you? Don't you have an ounce of sense?"

"Huh?" Kathlyn was still trying to calm herself after the fright David had given her.

"The music was blaring, the door unlocked. Anyone could have walked in here and done who knows what!"

She broke away from his clutch and stepped back, rubber hands on her hips. She spat out strands of the boa.

"You're the one who put me down here by myself.

I assumed you thought I was safe. It would have been nice to have informed me that I was in danger of being raped!''

David marched to the phone, furious. He was both frightened for her and aroused. ''Christine, send that kid Mike down to the storage room. Now! Tell him he'll be there until closing time today.'' He turned back to Kathlyn and . . . started laughing.

''What's so funny?''

Those monster hands were at the sides of her waist, the boa askew around her neck and in her disheveled hair. One sneakered foot tapped an angry tattoo, and her chest heaved under the words TEACHERS DO IT WITH CLASS.

''You.''

The fake hands came flying at him, the boa only making it a few inches. She turned her back and snatched the heads from the shelf. David edged toward the door.

Kathlyn was returning the items to their boxes when she heard the door open.

''If you have a couple of students who'd like a temporary job helping you, get them in here.''

''Yes, sir!''

''Smart mouth!''

''Dictator!''

''I'll, ah, pick you up for dinner at seven-thirty.''

Kathlyn was hiding her grin. ''Eight.''

The door closed on his chuckle.

Her two students began working the next day. Bill helped with the inventory while Sally transferred the information to the computer. Kathlyn unearthed a wonderful cache of children's toys and made up her mind to find a way to donate them to needy children.

On Sunday she took her turn as song leader at the ten-o'clock Mass. When David arrived at her place at eleven-thirty, he had to wait while she finished dressing. He was suddenly so relaxed that he almost fell asleep on her couch. What was it that made him unwind so completely the minute he stepped into her home? The rest of the week he'd tossed and turned and contrived business deals in his sleep. He was a wreck until he was near her. Then, for some reason, the whole world fell calmly into place.

He had tried to suppress a recent lone thought. It refused to go away. Falling in love? The idea made every nerve in his body jump to attention, but he felt a powerful longing to take Kathlyn as his wife. To love her and care for her, and have her care for him. No! He'd always taken care of himself. He always would. He couldn't let himself become dependent on anyone— especially for peace and happiness. He frowned, thinking of the pain marriage had caused his mother.

EIGHT

Damn, that woman filled out an innocent pair of shorts! The sleeveless tank top wasn't doing David's heart rate any good, either. All that lovely, golden skin, just waiting to be touched. If he made a commitment to her, he'd have the right to touch her. And she, him. The hair on his arms and legs stood up in anticipation.

They were sitting in Phil's backyard with a host of David's college buddies. The pungent aroma of steaks poured from the grill. High-pitched yells filled the air as children ran helter-skelter around the lawn. The heat of the sun, mixing with a playful breeze, made them all comfortable and lazy.

During the meal, David watched the children. Joe's two kids were fairly well behaved but ate like hogs from a trough. They continually giggled with their mouths full. Jim's boy was a brat. He kept pulling his little sister's pigtails when no adult was looking.

Pat's wife had finished feeding her baby right before they'd sat down to eat. The sight of the baby nursing at her mother's breast wouldn't leave David. He could picture Kathlyn nourishing her child. *Their* child? The picture conjured up wishfulness, longing, and a sense of fulfillment. He looked over at the baby now. The mother was eating with one hand, the baby sleeping peacefully on her shoulder. As David watched, the baby stirred, lifted her head, and spit up a glob of white goo. The mother didn't notice. David turned away with a heartfelt "Yuck!"

Babies! They cried and messed and spit up. Kids. They teased and fought and ran their parents ragged. Teenagers. David shuddered. He couldn't think of one good reason to bring a child into the world. He couldn't imagine how one of those would fit into his life, or why he would want one to.

He looked around at his friends. They all looked so content. No, *stodgy*, he corrected, knowing as he did that he was wrong. His friends didn't seem to mind a bunch of kids climbing all over them. They didn't seem to mind the responsibility of having to train these hellions to run the world. In fact, they looked downright smug about the whole thing!

Kathlyn lifted David's empty plate from his lap and kissed him before carting the plate off to the trash barrel. He sat back in the lawn chair and closed his eyes for a moment. He felt a soft tickle on the top of his bent leg and looked down into the clearest set of green eyes he'd ever seen.

"Hi," a little munchkin said.

"Hi, princess."

David smiled and was rewarded with a big, dimpled grin from the little girl. His gaze moved down to the pudgy, dimpled hand resting on his thigh between the hem of his navy shorts and his kneecap. Her hand moved again, skimming the hair on his leg. The princess sighed. The thumb of her other hand went into her cupid's bow mouth, and the next thing he knew, she was slowly rubbing her soft cheek over the hairs on his leg.

Goose bumps rose on his skin. A gigantic lump formed in his throat. He could no more stop himself from resting his hand on the baby's head, from moving his fingers in the soft down of her blond hair, than he could have stopped the moon from coming up. A slight understanding of his friends' smug looks entered his mind. A warm, cozy feeling entered his heart.

Kathlyn turned from the nearly cleared picnic table and saw David with the child. Her heart fluttered. Her love for him grew and solidified. At that moment she could picture David with their children.

The rest of the afternoon and into the evening, Kathlyn sat enthralled. More often than not, the spotlight fixed on David. Kathlyn found out that he had stretched his college years to four for social and academic reasons. He had wanted to take any subject and try any experience he thought interesting. Along the way, he'd gotten his master's in business.

At the beginning of his third year, David had turned himself over to some freshman girls to polish him up. Special task forces were assigned to clothing styles, colors, dancing and dating etiquette.

David leaned closer to Kathlyn and whispered, "And now, as they say, you know *the rest of the story*."

One of the men interrupted before Kathlyn could reply. "Hey, what about that move on the piano major?"

"That was no move," David cut in, a bright twinkle in his eyes. "She needed the money. I wanted to learn to play the piano."

"And did he ever!" another shouted. "The guy took six lessons, practiced every day for those six weeks, and played better than Liberace. Ever heard him play, Kathlyn?"

David's shoulders were silently shaking in laughter. Kathlyn knew something fishy was going on.

"How come I never heard you play?" Phil questioned indignantly.

David's shoulders shook harder. "You must have been busy or something."

"Come on, David, show them," they all urged.

David rose with a false air of embarrassment and led them into Phil's living room. He sat down at the baby grand and played the flashiest, liveliest version she'd ever heard of a Scott Joplin rag. Phil hooted and whistled, much impressed with David's expertise, but Kathlyn kept looking at David's face. There was something . . . Understanding flashed in her mind.

"Play another," she begged. David's head jerked up and caught the knowing look Kathlyn was flashing him. God, the woman was sharp! He grinned and turned back to the piano. He drastically slowed down the beat and altered the rhythm, but was playing the same tune.

Kathlyn and David and Phil broke into gales of laughter while the other men applauded and marveled at his genius.

In the car on their way home, Kathlyn teasingly shook her finger at him.

He shrugged his shoulders. "The girl did need the money from the lessons, and I wanted to learn to play. I practiced that song every day for six weeks. And I followed the piano tuner around and learned how to do that. It was fascinating."

Fascinating. That pretty much summed up David St. John. Fascinating, quick-witted, a genius—and the man she would love forever.

*   *   *

They left for Great Falls, Montana, on Monday morning, spending two days closing out a deal on the building of the mail-order house. From there they flew to Stockton, California, and spent Thursday and Friday checking out the production at a turkey ranch. Kathlyn wasn't much help out in the field. She was terrified of the fat gobblers. The incubators and tiny baby turkeys—poults—were tolerable, but she told him there was no way she'd waddle in the gunk where the live toms and hens were. And right there, while he was standing knee-deep in turkeys, calling out ideas through a megaphone for her to record, David fell solidly, wholeheartedly, in love with her.

On Saturday they drove over to Angels Camp, California, for the storm-delayed Calaveras County Frog Jumping Contest. The antics of the frogs' owners had them laughing even more than the wild frogs did.

From there they flew to Alaska and then down to the Mississippi coast. And between business meetings David wrestled with the fact that he honestly loved Kathlyn Marie McDaniel.

Back in Atlanta, Kathlyn, red-shouldered and red-nosed from the sun, went back to her basement warehouse and completed her listing. David took care of more paperwork and then went to visit his mother.

"Hi, Mom."

She was in the old family rocking chair, knitting. She looked up and smiled serenely. David could almost believe everything was normal.

"Oh, hi, David. How are you doing?"

"Just fine. Busy. What are you up to?"

Sarah laughed and held up the needles with their attached pink yarn. "Knitting. Or rather, making an attempt. Thought I'd give it a try to help fight off the arthritis beginning in these fingers."

Immediately alarmed, David asked, "Are you in pain?"

"No. Just trying to combat one of the things accompanying old age."

David studied his mother. She looked so old for someone only in her mid-fifties. His heart broke a little more, just as it did every time he visited her. "What are you making?"

"A baby afghan. I didn't want to try anything too complicated." She tilted her head to the side and studied the item. "You know, in the ordinary way of things, I could be knitting this for your child instead of for a charity baby." She sighed deeply. "It doesn't seem fair that you can never experience the joys of parenthood."

David pulled up a hassock and laid his folded hands across her knees. "Perhaps it's not all that impossible. Maybe I could work and lead a normal life. It'd be nice to have children." *And Kathlyn as a wife.*

The needles were immediately dropped, and her hands frantically clutched his. "Don't, David. Don't make that mistake. People like us can't combine the two. Your father told me today that he believes our lives would never have worked out. He deeply regretted that we let things go so far as to be married."

Bull! David wanted to shout it. Damn it all, his father was dead. How the hell did she know what her husband would have, should have, could have done if she'd been up-front with him? But no matter how hard he tried to fight for a dream he wanted to believe possible, he had the living proof in front of him as to what could happen. He couldn't do that to himself. Nor could he make Kathlyn's life as miserable and guilt-ridden as his father's had been after his mother was taken in for treatment.

During the last week of June, Kathlyn made phone calls to various companies to determine their interest in the novelty items. She typed up formal proposal letters and tried to figure out a way to keep from having to sell the children's toys.

David sat in his office and tried to concentrate on the papers in front of him. He finally pushed them aside and turned to stare out the window at the Atlanta skyline. Kathlyn. How the hell had she made her way into his heart so thoroughly? He had something like withdrawal symptoms whenever a day went by without his seeing her. He resented the hold she had on him, the fact that he loved her, and that his mother was most likely right. None of that, however, changed the way he missed her and needed to be with her.

Damn it. He wanted to know that she was his. That she wouldn't be going out looking for that husband she knew she would find. He, David St. John, wanted to be that husband.

The problem was that he had to be sure it could work. Once he made the commitment to marriage with Kathlyn, there was no backing out. No divorce. With Kathlyn he had to be positive from the start. She wouldn't marry again. Once married, always married. If he left her, she would spend the rest of her life alone.

The burden became unbearable, and he quickly left his desk. He told his secretary where he was going, left a message for Kathlyn, and took off for his grandfather's.

Kevin St. John was still spry for a man close to eighty, but his limp, his arthritic hands, and the many lines in the old man's dear face told David he wouldn't be around much longer. David rebelled at the thought.

"Why didn't you marry again after Grandmother's death?" David asked as they strolled the grounds.

Kevin stopped walking, and both men leaned against a pasture fence. The horses were no longer Kevin's, but their stately gaits and shiny coats were familiar. It irritated him that he was no longer capable of doing some of the things he enjoyed most, but not as much as it would some. In the not-too-distant future he would finally join his Maggie.

"Because I never loved anyone else the way I loved her." He and David had never talked about loving and wives. Perhaps he could leave this world knowing that David had found the same bliss that he had.

"Sometimes there's only one woman for a man. No one else will do. Your grandmother and I were such a pair. A pair of idiots, sometimes." He laughed, remembering the silly antics they had engaged in. "She was my support, my driving force, my love. My life. I like to think I was the same for her."

Like Kathlyn? David thought. He hated being so torn and confused—wanting to believe he was not like his mother, knowing his mother believed he was. And he hated not knowing how to find out without actually marrying.

"I met a woman. What I feel about her is causing me a lot of grief."

Kevin laughed. "Women'll do that."

"No. She's not ornery like Grandma. The grief is all within me. She needs a commitment, Grandpa. She needs a man who's stable, who'll stay with her for the rest of her life."

"And that ain't you?" Kevin was shocked that David doubted his own staying ability. Hell, the kid was as stable as they came. He was the one who had held his father together after his mother's breakdown.

"I don't know. I just don't know, damn it. And then there's the thing about having kids. What kind of a father would I make?"

"I seem to remember a little boy of about eleven ranting and raving about the beatings one of his classmates received at home. About a high school buddy of yours whose father kept pushing him into sports when all he wanted to do was play the violin. You said, and I quote, 'When I get to be a father, I'm going to do a hell of a better job than those parents.' "

But, David wondered, would he be around enough to be a good father, or would his constantly searching mind cause him to neglect his family?

David pushed himself away from the fence and began walking again. None of this was getting him anywhere. He had to fight his own demons. Giants, he corrected.

The old man limped beside him. "Who's the girl?"

David smiled. "Her name's Kathlyn Marie McDaniel. She recently studied to be a nun."

"Hmmm," the old man mumbled as he rubbed his hand across his stubbled chin. "Could it be sex, or the lack thereof, that's pushing you into thinking about marriage?"

"Is that what drove you to marry Grandma?"

"Hell, no. I didn't want anyone but her."

"You've had others since she died."

"Watch your mouth, boy. That was only need. And"—he wagged a finger under David's nose—"none of them came close to Maggie."

"Yeah, I know. I'm just not interested in anyone else. But I don't think that's all it is. In fact, I know that's not all there is to my wanting her. She—don't you repeat this to another soul—she makes me feel content, peaceful. As if everything's okay with the whole damn world as long as she's around.''

Kevin sighed. ''Yes. That's how it feels.''

Both men strolled back to the house. One deep in memories, the other in dreams of the future.

David stayed at the homestead for two more days, walking and thinking, watching and talking to his grandfather. At the end of the two days David knew that he didn't want to die without having known the joys of belonging to one woman. What he didn't know, yet, was whether he could take the plunge, with its risk of failure, with Kathlyn.

Before leaving, David did something he had not done nearly enough in his lifetime. He hugged his grandfather fiercely and whispered, ''I love you.'' And it wasn't so hard to hug and say the words, to let someone know how he felt. He had spent too long trying not to feel, trying not to acknowledge his deeper emotions. Love. He loved his mom. He loved his grandpap. He loved Kathlyn. And by loving, he was . . . vulnerable.

After boarding the plane the next week, David watched Kathlyn do her work. His own lay untouched on his lap. He grinned at her intensity and determination. God, the woman was a dream—his dream.

Marriage? He thought the word with only a slight quiver. He had tried to stay away from her to sort himself out, to shore up his vulnerability. He had limited his visits to office hours. That didn't mean, however, that he had been able to limit his kisses. He had taken one, sometimes two, every time he had visited her. He sighed deeply and shut his eyes.

The nights had been the worst. He had dreamed of her, sometimes waking up smiling, other times sweating in a sexual fever. Once, he had been startled awake from a nightmare of having to tell her that their relationship was over. He'd walked around his apartment fuming and swearing at himself. Here he was, genius, Mensa member, highly successful career person, and in social adaptability he was still years behind most men.

When he did see her, his heart always flipped and then settled comfortably. Why couldn't his relationships with women be as smooth as in business? Why did his brain turn to jelly every time he was around her?

Kathlyn pulled out the papers she had brought along to study. She calculated how much money they'd have if the promised sales went through. She furiously wrote down plans for a big garage sale for the remaining items, and designed and set up the advertisements she would send out. There was still a deficit. Since David had finally explained that the proceeds were going to the man who originally owned the company, and that that man needed the money to support his family, Kathlyn knew she had to make up that deficit.

She suddenly hit on the idea for raising the remaining funds. She turned to tell David, then caught herself before she woke him. Poor man. He worked so hard to make sure that all parties in the transactions were satisfied. He had barely had time to spend with her, and she had missed him terribly. If it hadn't been for those knee-knocking kisses he gave her, she would have thought he was trying to end what was between them.

And what was that? It was already the first week in July, and she felt as if they had not progressed at all toward the ultimate end. She loved him more than she'd ever thought it possible to love, but he was acting exactly as he had before the summer started. Kathlyn knew it was more than friendship, that he still wanted her sexually. But that's where they had been in May.

Her patience was wearing thin. In six weeks she had to go back to school. Would David feel differently then?

It took him two weeks to straighten out the mess at the commercial dairy farm in the southern New York Appalachian Plateau. At the end of the two weeks, all local, state, and federal regulations were once again being followed, the Holstein cows' records were up-to-date, and the herd had been weeded out.

Kathlyn was awed by David's knowledge, and extremely impressed by his take-charge ability. She was also exhausted. She ate little that Friday night, and flopped into bed while the sun was still shining.

The next day David bundled her into a rental car and sped down Highway 15, claiming they needed a little recreation. They entered Bath, a small New York town of a little over six thousand people, early enough to get a good spot for the annual Christmas in July parade. The excited voices of the shorts-clad children mixed harmoniously with Christmas carols. Kathlyn sucked on a candy cane thrown to her by a live doll on one of the floats, and when Santa and his entourage rode by she grinned and waved and blew him a kiss, which was returned with a jolly "Ho, ho, ho!" After the parade, she and David strolled hand in hand through the town, window-shopping mostly, and admiring the Christmas decorations in each storefront. It was hot, as un-Christmas-like as possible, but the feeling was of peace on earth and goodwill toward men.

When she came out of one of the stores with a Christmas present for David, a tree ornament of a cow, she saw him talking to a nice-looking gentleman of perhaps six feet, with blond hair and a tanned, healthy complexion. Next to David, he was bland.

"Kathlyn." David held out a hand for her to join

them. "I'd like you to meet Alex VanHorn. Alex, my secretary, Kathlyn McDaniel."

His secretary? Was that all she was to him? Kathlyn turned a polite face to Alex, but her heart had snapped in two. After all this time and all they had shared, couldn't he at least have introduced her as his friend?

"Nice to meet you, Ms. McDaniel. David, your taste is getting better all the time. The last secretary I met was about five feet in all directions. Kathlyn, darlin', would you like to join me in a drink this hot afternoon?" He nodded toward a soft drink stand.

"Yes, I would like something cool. What would you like, David? A glass of water?" *Poured over your thick head?*

"A beer would go down just fine about now."

David watched the two of them walk away arm in arm. Arm in arm? Well, damn! What the hell right did Alex have horning in on *his* girl? That old playboy wouldn't understand the first thing about Kathlyn and her faith and angels and statues that were talked to. Not like he did. Stunned, David inhaled a deep breath.

He was going to do it—he was going to ask Kathlyn to marry him! All of his adult life he had wanted what he thought he could never have—marriage and a family. Deep down, buried but not always forgotten, had been the knowledge that he needed those things. Hadn't Kathlyn searched within herself to come up with the same conclusion? Damn it, somehow he would make it work. He wasn't his mother!

But . . . what if she didn't want to marry him? David sat down on a bench so abruptly that he jarred his spine. What if he wasn't her Mr. Right? While he had been plodding along trying to figure out if he should or could marry her, was she hoping for someone else? He had assumed that if he finally got up the nerve to ask her, she would marry him. What a pompous ass!

When Kathlyn sat down next to David, surrounding him in that exquisite wildflower fragrance, he put his arm around her possessively, hoping that old lecher Alex would move on to other conquests. After a few minutes of polite chitchat, Alex stood up and grinned at David in a peculiar way. David frowned at him but politely shook hands.

The minute Alex left, David removed his arm from Kathlyn's shoulder. "Did he ask you out?"

"Yes."

"We won't be around long enough for you to start anything." His words sounded hostile to Kathlyn.

Darn it all. If she was only a secretary to him, she'd go out with someone else if she wanted to! "I don't know what's gotten into you, David, but whether or not I go out with Alex isn't any of your business."

That's what you think! "He's not good enough for you."

Oh, great! Now he was acting like a big brother. Just what she needed.

"Are you dating anyone in Atlanta?"

His question made Kathlyn angrier. "No. But Sandra's brother has called a couple of times."

"Do you think he's the one?"

"David, I don't know what you want from me!" She was almost in tears. How could he talk about her dating other men when she was waiting for him to admit that he loved her? He sounded as if he was trying to tell her the opposite.

"Hell." The word exploded from his lips. His hand rifled through his curly hair.

What was he so agitated about? She was the one who

should be wailing and beating her head against a rock. Or better yet, beating his head against one.

"I was wondering if you were still looking for that husband you want. Is Sandra's brother the one?"

Kathlyn took a deep breath and let it out slowly, hoping that her tears would stay blocked up. "He might be one of the forty thousand, but I don't love him. I guess it could grow into something comfortable, but I really haven't been looking anymore."

"What do you feel about me?"

How was she supposed to answer that without scaring him off? Unless . . . "Do you really want to know?"

"Yes."

She actually heard him gulp. Was he frightened that she'd say she didn't love him, or that she'd say she did? She was scared. Scared that when he heard her answer he'd run faster than the reindeer flew on Christmas eve.

"I think you're the grand passion of my life." Her mouth went bone-dry. She quickly took a sip of her drink.

David's head was spinning. Her grand passion! God, he felt as if the roller coaster he was on had left its tracks and was hurtling thrillingly out into space. Her grand passion! She was going to be his! He turned on the bench and kissed her hard and long and deep. He played with her tongue and tasted the delicious orange pop still in her mouth. It fizzled against his tongue. Good God, she was his!

Ask her. Not yet. Ask her. I will, but I have to be sure. Now shut up and let me kiss her.

Kathlyn didn't care about the place or the people watching them. After her announcement, not only hadn't he gone running, but he had snatched her up in a possessive embrace. She tasted joy and what she hoped was love in his kiss, and kissed him back with all the love she had.

He withdrew from the kiss, but came back again and again for little nibbles that had Kathlyn begging for more. The crowd around them clapped and cheered. David let out a deep belly laugh and stood and bowed to them. He grabbed Kathlyn's hand and pulled her along with him down the decorated street.

He didn't say anything more about her declaration that afternoon. Nor that evening. Nor on their flight to Washington, D.C. Kathlyn sensed she could only settle back into her waiting game, waiting for her world to explore or finally settle into place.

In the Capitol, she followed David right into one of the Senate chambers and sat in on a discussion between senators, representatives, and David. She took notes and listened as some of the most renowned men in politics questioned David about an antipollution device he'd invented. She tried to keep her mouth from opening when she was introduced to the men and as she listened to David explain the device. When it was all over, they joined the senator from Georgia for dinner. She went to sleep that night more proud of the man she loved than ever.

The next two days they toured the Smithsonian. They could have spent weeks there. To their curious minds, the place was a treasure trove. Would David's antipollution device be in here one day, as a forerunner of those to come? More than once Kathlyn watched as David studied some invention, some contraption. Sometimes they stood for fifteen, twenty minutes while David muttered, "What if . . ." or "Suppose . . ." After the first time, Kathlyn took a small notebook from her purse and jotted down his suppositions.

On the last day of their visit, David again took her

someplace unusual—the National Herb Garden. They roamed through the Knot Garden, once fashionable in Elizabethan England, the Historic Rose Garden, with species used for medicine, perfume, food, and pleasure.

Finally, right in the middle of the Fragrance Garden, surrounded by the scents of rosemary, sage, and thyme, David took hold of Kathlyn's hands and placed them under his on his chest. She could feel the thumping of his heart. He leaned close to her. Anticipating a kiss, Kathlyn leaned closer to him.

"Kathlyn Marie McDaniel, my love, will you marry me?"

NINE

David had spoken the words she had prayed to hear. Tears of intoxicating joy filled Kathlyn's eyes, and she nodded. "Oh, yes!"

She reached up and pulled his head down for a sweet meeting of lips, a sharing of love. She peppered his face with little pecks. "Yes, David, I would be honored to marry you."

He cupped his hands around her face and brought his lips to hers in a kiss of hunger and relief. He raised his head and slanted his mouth over hers from a different angle, deepening the kiss and sending Kathlyn's appetite soaring. She could live off the taste of him, could die from the hunger he built in her. She wrapped her hands around his strong neck. His hands encircled her, pulling her as close to his hard, welcoming body as he could. When his hands dropped to her buttocks and rubbed her lower body against his flaming need, she reveled in the knowledge that she could do this to him, that she wanted him as much as he wanted her.

And, dear sweet heaven, their final joining was going to happen! She found it difficult to hold back her desires. Her body burned, her breasts filled and ached, and a tingling fever flared between her legs. She helplessly rubbed herself against his arousal, knowing somehow that her need for total capitulation was nearly impossible to stop.

Moisture dotted her face, a few irritating drops at first, and then what seemed an entire bucketful. Their lips separated, and slowly the world came back into focus. Birds squawked overhead, and the pungent aroma of the Fragrance Garden filled Kathlyn's nostrils. Together they looked up at the sky. One lonely cloud seemed to be pouring its contents right on their heads, soaking them. They started to laugh, a laugh of joy and anticipation of what was to come in their lives. David grabbed Kathlyn and hugged her hard. Lifting her off her feet, he spun her around in the rain. Kathlyn looked heavenward and mouthed a heartfelt thank-you.

David was giddy with happiness. God, he loved this woman! With her securely wrapped under his arm, they zigzagged through the gardens. When they reached the car, the cloudburst had ended. Fitting his silly grin over hers, he gave her a smacking kiss and then put her in the car. Nothing had ever felt as right for him as this. Fears or not, he was going to make it work!

She sat as close to him as her seat belt allowed. He drove with one hand, not wanting to lose contact. The wet material of her short-sleeved jacket rubbed against his arm, as did the pointed nipple beneath the material. His senses, already inflamed from their kisses, soared. Good God! Once he married her, they were going to make love. It was what he'd wanted from the moment he'd met her, but until today it had been an impossible dream. Wanting and not being able to have her had been difficult. Now, knowing he was going to have her was going to make the waiting far beyond difficult.

They made it up to their suite with only a minimum of touching and kissing. David reluctantly parted from her in the sitting area, watching her until she entered her room before going to his bedroom to get out of his wet clothes.

Kathlyn removed her jacket and draped it over the bathroom doorknob. Her knees began to shake. She was going to marry David St. John! She wobbled to the colonial bed and sat down on the edge of the patchwork spread. In spite of her conviction about him being the one, the reality of it left her stunned.

"Isn't it wonderful, Mary?" Her voice trembled, and her lips still burned from his kisses. "I'll do all right, won't I? Is lovemaking as wonderful as they say? Will the pain give way to the sweet joy of climax? Will our love produce children? I'll try to be a good wife and mother. That's all God asks, isn't it?"

She stood up and removed her bra. "Oh, Mary, I love him so much."

Her bedroom door flew open and David came in. "Who were you talking . . . no, don't cover yourself. Please, angel, let me look."

Kathlyn's hands slowly dropped from her breasts, and David looked, taking his fill. She was far more beautiful than he'd imagined. And yes, she was golden all over. Her nipples, puckered from the cold or desire, were that dusky rose color he loved to watch creep into her cheeks when she blushed. He didn't look up to see if she was blushing now; he couldn't tear his gaze away from her breasts. He stepped closer and then closer until he was finally able to reach out a hand and touch her. He closed his eyes and savored the feel of her fullness in his palm. He cupped one breast and then raised his other hand to fondle the mate. He kneaded and smoothed his hands over the full, firm mounds.

His thumbs moved slowly until they skimmed over her puckered nipples. He heard Kathlyn's gasp and opened his eyes. Lord, she was radiant. Her face was flushed and her eyes were dilated with passion.

"Is this so you won't be completely surprised on our wedding night?" Her voice was a mere thread of sound, lower and sexier than he'd ever heard it.

His own voice shook nearly as much as his hands. "Something like that."

He reached up and unbuttoned the fresh shirt he had just put on. He glided his hands along her smooth flesh until they met at her back, and then he pulled her forward until her nipples were lost in the patch of hair on his chest. His flesh burned where those pointed peaks burrowed into him. He shuddered, and she gave a quivery sigh and melted against him. He lowered his head and kissed her tenderly. Then slowly—very, very slowly—he began moving her from side to side against his chest. He shuddered again and devoured her mouth hungrily. He could taste her sweetness, taste her desire, taste her surrender. His body cried out for release. He prayed for control.

Kathlyn pressed her breasts harder against his chest and moved more strongly against him. "David," she begged.

He knew what she wanted better than she did. The knowledge that he was the first to see her like this made his head spin. With great care he moved her away from his body. She cried out her disappointment. He lowered his head and took an extended nipple into his mouth. When he heard her again cry out, this time in desire, he almost exploded. She grabbed his head, pulling him tighter against her breast, begging him not to stop. He managed to move from her strong hold just enough to capture the other nipple and slip it into his mouth. His tongue lapped at the swollen point over and over, and Kathlyn went into climax. Surprised at her responsiveness, David automatically tried to pull away. Her grip was so strong, he couldn't break it.

When the climax ended, Kathlyn's breathing was labored. David focused on her face. She glowed like an ethereal being. Her eyes were a deep cobalt blue, the light in them so bright, he was almost blinded. He pulled her roughly against him and held her tightly, knowing they couldn't continue.

His arousal did not pass quickly, but when it finally did, it left him weak. He sat her on the edge of the bed, bent, and gave each one of her nipples a tender parting kiss. Then he straightened rather awkwardly and left the room.

Kathlyn flopped backwards onto the bed, hugging a pillow close to her racing heart. Once her thinking powers returned, she lifted her eyes back to heaven. "I think I'll do all right."

A firm knock on the bedroom door was followed immediately by David's voice. "Quit talking to all your friends up there, angel, and get your sweet self in gear. I think we'd better head back to Atlanta this evening."

Yes, perhaps they should. She rose and began removing the rest of her wet clothes. For the first time in her life she completely understood the temptation of sex.

"When would you like to get married?" Kathlyn asked on the way to the airport.

"Perhaps it would be better to wait until I get my business affairs in order. It shouldn't take more than two months." He couldn't believe he had said that. Two more months without making her his. But once his business was taken care of, he'd have more time to devote to loving her.

"That's fine. After working for you, I'm sure I can handle planning a wedding and teaching."

He'd forgotten that she would be going back to school. "When do you start?"

"In about a month. The date is sometime in mid August."

And then what? Once she started back to school, he'd be doing his traveling alone or with another secretary. Since he had first seen Kathlyn, he hadn't wanted another woman, but what if that old craving for a new challenge came over him while she was in Atlanta and he was out in the field? What if he became so involved in what he was doing, he forgot about her completely?

Hesitantly he asked, "Would you consider taking a leave of absence for this year? That way you could still travel with me, and we could have a year of sharing. A year of just the two of us."

Compromise. That's what marriage was all about. A year together would help cement their marriage. "Okay. I think that's fair. I'll talk to the superintendent when we get back. He should be able to find another music teacher by the time school starts."

"Thanks, love. Are you sure?"

"I'm sure." She leaned over and kissed him. "I'll also make an appointment for us with Father Flynn."

Us? David's stomach churned.

"It's nothing to worry about. Honestly."

David figured he'd find out one way or the other.

At work the next day, Kathlyn called the superintendent of her school district. He wasn't pleased to hear she wanted a leave of absence, but after reminding her that since she was not tenured, there would be no pay, he granted her leave.

Her next call was to Alex VanDorn. She had found out that he was a wealthy playboy skimming his way along the surface of life. Cutting through his banter, she finally convinced him to buy the children's toys and give them to poor children.

She arranged for the advertising and got the ball rolling for her garage sale and then called the rectory to set up an appointment with Father Flynn. She could have seen the assistant pastor, but decided to wait until Father Flynn got back from his vacation. David was leery of priests, but she knew he and Father Flynn would hit it off.

While she was at it, she canceled teaching CCD classes the next term. Hopefully she'd still be able to substitute when she was in town. Sadly, she also had to drop out as a regular song leader for the Masses. It wasn't comfortable, this abandoning all that had been in her life before David. But it also wasn't the first time she had had to go through something like it. Sometimes she felt as if her whole life was a series of starting over. Maybe everyone's was. She shrugged away the uncomfortable feelings and thought about life as David's wife.

On Saturday David took Kathlyn shopping for her rings. She wanted a simple wedding band, but David insisted on more. He wanted his brand on her finger. Surely he had meant *band*, hadn't he? At the fourth store he finally settled on a beautiful diamond-and-sapphire engagement ring and an interlocking wedding band, also with diamonds and sapphires. The rings were beautiful and symbolized everything she had prayed for. When he placed the engagement ring on her finger, Kathlyn cried.

She put her ring for David on layaway, since she couldn't afford it all at once. She was determined David was not going to walk around with a cheap symbol of her love.

They stopped at the local deli for foot-long sandwiches. Halfway through his, David sighed deeply and put down the rest.

"What's the matter?"

"Just tired, angel. I'm so exhausted that I can barely put one foot in front of the other. I can't sleep, and I don't feel like eating much. Would you mind if I came and stayed with you for a couple of days? I might even need you to play the cello for me. How about it, love?"

"You've stayed before. You know you're welcome anytime."

"Yeah, but we weren't engaged then. If anyone sees me, they'll think we're sleeping together."

When he'd met her, his whole purpose had been to get her into bed. The man definitely had come a long way.

"Let's go." She stood and held out her hand to him. He left some bills on the table and took her hand in his.

As they were leaving the building, a buxom blonde bumped into David. "Sorry. Are you all right?"

"Fine," the woman simpered.

David nodded.

Kathlyn looked back at the woman, who was staring wistfully at David. She had a feeling that the old David, dead on his feet or not, would have responded to the woman. The new David didn't even notice her. Kathlyn glowed from the inside out. Oh, yes, David was definitely in love with her. And he seemed to have no more fears about being nonmarriage material.

Once inside her apartment, Kathlyn made herbal tea while David removed his shoes and settled back on the couch. He sipped the tea while she played Chopin. During the Debussy he fell sound asleep.

When he awoke it was pitch dark. He stretched and

grinned and then turned on the lamp in order to see his watch. He was shocked that he had slept solidly for twelve hours. He tiptoed into Kathlyn's room. She lay on her back, the sheet around her waist. Her arms were flung over her head, making the bodice of her cotton nightgown cling and reveal what he so badly wanted to see and touch. Mine, he thought as he fought with himself not to join her in her warm cocoon. He sat on the edge of the bed.

She stirred and opened her eyes. "Yes?" she said dreamily.

"What time are your church services?" he said, surprising himself. "I'd like to go with you."

"Church?" Her mind had been on the bedroom. "There's a Mass at eight, and ten. You pick."

"Eight. And then we'll go out for breakfast. Now, kiss me and let me go home."

Kathlyn leaned sleepily up on one elbow and kissed him. She really wanted to drag him down onto the bed with her, but knew by the dark glow in his eyes that she'd better not tempt either fate or David. "See you later."

"I'll set your alarm before I go." He leaned down and kissed her one more time.

After Mass they loaded their plates at Shoney's breakfast bar and sat across from each other in a booth. All around them were other early morning diners—a group of teenagers paired off in couples, older men and women dressed in their Sunday finery, groups of families enjoying a Sunday outing. And he, David, was a part of it. Finally, part of it.

He turned to Kathlyn, dressed in a soft pink shirt-dress. "At Mass you all stand up, sit down, and kneel a lot." He had felt like a foreigner, not knowing when to do what.

"It all has meaning. After a while it gets to be routine."

Routine. A ritualistic routine. Not necessarily a bad thing. David had enjoyed the meaning of the prayers. He had watched as most of the people recited them with deep fervor. The Mass had been a celebration of community, one that might be worth repeating.

That night they made a chicken dish for dinner. Well, Kathlyn did most of the making while David did his best to hug and kiss her.

When he nibbled on her neck, she laughed and ducked out of his way. "It's almost ready. Why don't you set the table?"

The wine was nectar of the gods, the chicken divine, and David devoured every bit of both. Sharing their time, the chores, and sitting at the table with her had him honestly believing that he had found a home. That he could be a vital part of the home. He wanted to share. "I'd like you to meet my grandpap."

Kathlyn's eyes lit up. "The ornery one?"

"Ornery, opinionated, bullheaded. The best damn grandpap in the whole world."

Kathlyn's grin widened. "It'll be a pleasure taking you both on."

David stood and threw down his napkin. He moved threateningly toward her and scooped her up into his arms. "I'm not sure you can handle one of us, much less two. Don't get too sure of yourself, girl."

Kathlyn looped her arms around his neck and played with the curls there. His eyes dilated. "I think I can handle it."

"Said the little engine who could."

He lowered his head, and Kathlyn raised hers for a longed-for kiss. This time the sweet caress turned wild almost immediately. She returned his hunger and his need.

She didn't know how they ended up on the couch with her lying beneath his firm body, but she did know when he unbuttoned the bodice of her dress and unsnapped her bra. When he kissed and teased her tender breasts, when he opened his shirt and rubbed the curly hairs on his chest over her nipples, she was lost in sensations, in loving David and loving what he did to her. She wasn't aware that he had raised the lower half of her dress until his frank arousal nestled against her. For one brief moment of complete abandon, she wanted to rip the thin material of her panties aside and welcome him. She almost begged him to strip her all the way and join them as they were meant to be joined.

She opened her glazed eyes and watched him raise his head. As his eyes, closed in ecstasy, opened, suddenly his muscles stiffened. He collapsed on top of her. His breath was hot and heavy against her neck.

She knew what he had seen. The statue of Mary had stopped him, right where he should have stopped.

"Sorry." His breath was rapid against her neck. A thrilling chill covered her body. "I'm so sorry."

After a few more deep breaths, he lifted himself onto his forearms. He looked down at her near nudity and groaned out loud.

Kathlyn lifted a limp hand and stroked his cheek. "I feel the same way, but you know what? I think we just proved that we're going to be dynamite in bed."

David kissed her nose. "I think you just uttered the understatement of the year. Now, get up and cover yourself." He lifted himself off her and strode into the dining room to tote dishes to the kitchen. "I can't believe how wanton you are. Imagine taking advantage of a houseguest that way. Shame, shame."

A throw pillow landed smack against the back of his head. David laughed and continued with the cleanup chores. He did take a peek around the corner of the kitchen to watch her redress. It was almost as erotic as watching her undress. However, he could tell that she wasn't all that comfortable with what had gone on between them. He walked over to her and raised her chin so she'd look at him.

"Listen to me. I can't control the reaction of my body to yours, but I can control what I do about it. I am not going to make love to you until we're married. What we did just now is all right. There is nothing to be embarrassed about. I love your response to me. I love the way I respond to you." He kissed her sweetly. "I love you. Okay?"

"Okay." She smiled at him and kissed him.

David walked back to the dining room whistling. They gathered up the plates and then he turned to her. "You do know that after a few years of marriage, the sexual urge calms down?"

"It does?"

"That's what I've read. However"—he loomed over her dramatically—"a great deal of our time during that first year will be spent setting fires like the one we started, and putting them out."

Kathlyn looked straight into his eyes. "Promise?"

"Promise. It's going to be good, angel. So damn good! When do we go to see the priest?"

"Next Wednesday afternoon. You are free, aren't you?"

Hell, he'd change his entire schedule to be free. He wanted this wedding a fait accompli. In fact, two months was definitely going to be too long to wait.

He slept at Kathlyn's three nights that week and went with her on Saturday for her garage sale. He was amazed at her organizational skills and the way she pulled off something he'd never thought would succeed. By three o'clock that afternoon, everything except a few broken items was sold. He congratulated her and gave her the next two weeks off.

On Monday Kathlyn went shopping for a bridal gown. She fell in love with one at the first store she entered. It was a lightweight satin gown straight from the nineteenth century. It had a slightly belled skirt, short sleeves, high neck, and bustle. To go with it she purchased a saucy hat, a chapeau really, with the brim curled up on one side. She stood before the dressing room mirror, awed, her stomach fluttering. Her eyes and her flushed cheeks glowed. She could hardly wait for David to see her in the outfit.

David didn't spend Monday or Tuesday night at her apartment, and Kathlyn missed him. She missed sharing meals, but mostly she missed their steamy good-night kisses.

On Tuesday David visited with his mother. He didn't know why she'd kept harping on his not getting married during the past month. Could she see into his heart? He had dreaded coming this evening and had considered telling her about Kathlyn and his wedding plans. He wanted to ease her into it before he brought Kathlyn to visit. He changed his mind. In fact, he lost his temper with his mother, telling her that since she had screwed up her own life so badly, she should just stay the hell out of his. He didn't wait for a reply. He didn't want to see how much he hurt her.

On Wednesday afternoon he picked up Kathlyn for their appointment with the priest. David greeted her as if he had not seen her in months. He'd been shaken after yesterday, beginning to have doubts again after only two days away from her. But once he saw her, held her, kissed her, the doubts were soothingly blanketed.

His nerves, however, were on edge by the time they drove up to the rectory. Suppose the priest demanded that he become a Catholic? What would his choices be? Would he have any? Did he need Kathlyn so much that he'd do anything, sacrifice anything, to keep her? When the rectory door closed behind him, David felt trapped.

Trapped?

Marriage is a trap, son. Don't let anyone, not even someone you love, keep you from doing what you have to do.

His father's words, echoing his mother's, shot through David's mind like a lightning bolt. NO. They didn't mean anything. They were simply the ravings of a sick old man, of a poor confused woman.

David wiped the perspiration from his brow. Kathlyn wouldn't trap him. She wouldn't prevent him from doing what he had to do. She had given him her support and encouragement during these last months. He loved her. But then, hadn't his parents thought they were in love?

"David, I'd like you to meet Father Michael Flynn. Father, my fiancé, David St. John."

Good God, the man was built like a linebacker! Priests weren't supposed to be six foot six and over 250 pounds. The priest's hand engulfed David's. His eyes bored into David's as if studying him under a microscope.

Trapped!

David's hands were sweating as he followed Kathlyn and the priest into the office.

"Excuse me, but could I use your bathroom?" David hoped his voice sounded calm. Never before had he been this close to screaming.

Father Michael looked at David. There was something more here than the usual case of bridegroom jitters. "It's down the hall. First door on the left."

He watched David leave and tried to hide his frown. He'd known Kathlyn since she had come to Atlanta, and had helped her get settled and start over. When he'd heard the news from his secretary, he had been curious about the man she had decided to marry. To say that he'd been surprised was an understatement. How had a man like St. John hooked up with the sweet innocent in front of him? And why did the man look as if he were approaching the gallows?

David leaned against the sink in the bathroom, staring sightlessly into the white porcelain. *Marriage is a trap, David. Don't let it happen to you. You've too much to offer the world to let a woman hold you back.*

The words echoed in David's head. He didn't want to believe them.

"I want to marry her. She loves me. I love her." His whispered words rebounded off the white bathroom walls.

He took a deep breath and shoved away from the sink. He wanted to be with Kathlyn. Everything would be fine if he didn't let her become an overwhelming need. They loved each other. They were not his parents.

He repeated the sentences like a litany as he left the bathroom and reentered the rectory office. He sat in the chair in front of the desk and next to Kathlyn. He reached across the narrow chasm and clasped her hand in his.

"So, David, you plan to marry our little Kathlyn?"

"Yes, sir, uh, Father." David straightened in his chair. "I do intend to." There! That sounded like he meant it!

"Why?"

"Because I love her."

Michael looked deep into David's eyes. Yes, the man loved her. And desired her, he added, recognizing that look, too. This couple would share a wonderful love life, just as he and his sweet wife, Mary, had done before he became a priest. How he had missed her for the ten long years since her death. He glanced at Kathlyn and saw the love shining out of her eyes as she looked at David. Oh, yes, this couple loved each other, but . . . David was still troubled about something. Deeply troubled.

"The first thing I want you two to do is take a psychology test to show that you're compatible and have the same goals in your marriage. After that we'll get down to the details."

David moved to a chair in the corner of the room and looked at the test. He saw the words *sex, children, spouse, finances, church, Christ*. He felt the knot of tension coil tighter within him. He saw the phrase *pledge love under all circumstances*. How far was that meant to be carried? He read the word *need*, and his mind fogged over in a red haze. He began filling out the test. He'd taken many psychology tests through the years, had even helped design a couple of them. He knew which answers were expected of him. He started filling in circles.

Any circles.

Except the right ones.

Father Michael took the sheets from them and placed them on his desk. "I'll put these through the computer later, and let you know the results at our next meeting. David, some simple instruction in our beliefs is required of you. Only so that you can better understand where Kathlyn is coming from." David's look of irritation made Michael angry. What was wrong with the man? If he didn't want to marry Kathlyn, a woman so strongly rooted in faith, why was he here? He was going to hurt her.

"The waiting period is six months, and a marriage preparation course of six weeks is required. You can call my secretary to find out when the next class is scheduled." As he had expected, David sagged with relief about the six months and looked belligerent at the mention of the classes. Kathlyn was going to be devastated when this man proved himself incompatible. Well, better now, before the marriage, than after.

As he and David shook hands, Michael's anger dissipated. David looked miserably frightened. Sympathy welled up. "If you want to talk," he said so that Kathlyn could not hear, "call any time."

Michael went to Kathlyn and kissed her cheek. *Please, dear Lord, help her.*

David breathed in the fresh air outside the rectory as if he had just been released from prison. He took the hand Kathlyn extended to him, amazed when she said, "Now, that wasn't so bad, was it?"

Maybe not for her, with her rosy ideas of married life. Happily ever after with a houseful of children. And David tied down to them all.

Forever. Or until he broke under the chains.

"I'm sorry about the six months, David. I thought the long waiting period was for younger couples not sure about the step they were taking."

His half of the couple was definitely not sure! God, he was going to hurt her. He didn't want to. He loved her. Yes, damn it, he loved her!

"It's okay," he said as they entered her apartment. He looked at the statue. He recalled all Father Michael had said about instructions and classes. He remembered the questions on the test. And he heard his parents' warning again.

Trapped! By his need for her. He was not meant to marry. Kathlyn turned in to his arms and hugged him. "I love you, David," she whispered into his ear. "And I promise to love you and cherish you and take care of you, body and soul, for the rest of our lives."

Body and soul. For the rest of their lives. *Trapped.*

He broke away from her encircling arms, suddenly furious with himself, his parents, and Kathlyn. "Damn it all. You already control my mind. Most of my business decisions are based on what you'd have me do. My body is no longer my own, reacting to you nearly every minute of every day. And now you want my soul? No way. It's my soul. Whether it's damned or not is no one's business but mine!"

He raked his hand through his hair. He paced and then turned back to her, blazingly angry. "Marriage *is* a trap. A trap where one person tries to control the other. But I'm in charge of my life, and you cannot, I will not let you, take control of it. By damn, I kicked the habit of smoking, and I'll do the same with you."

He saw the stricken look on her face, watched as helpless tears filled her eyes and ran down her cheeks. He couldn't bear it, so he turned his back to her. "I'm calling it off, Kathlyn. I want no part of marriage. I told you a long time ago that I wasn't the marrying kind. I honestly thought I could do it with you. I was mistaken. I'll never tie myself to a woman who demands everything I have."

He stormed to the door. He had just put his hand on the knob when he heard Kathlyn's choked, tearful voice. "And I think, David, that I'm the best thing that ever happened to you."

He flung open the door and slammed it shut behind

him. Who did she think she was, telling him that she was his salvation?

The awful thing about it was that she was probably right!

TEN

"David!" Kathlyn called after him. Her heart was pounding, her stomach knotting. Dear God, what had happened? She had had her dream within sight. Everything had been glorious, and then . . . Why? Because she wanted to take care of him body and soul? No, there was something more, something deeper.

She stood facing the closed door for another long moment, tears streaming down her face. He *couldn't* be gone. He wouldn't leave her. But, dear heaven, he had!

She turned and rushed blindly toward the only solid thing in her life right now. She cried and hugged her statue until the evening shadows darkened the room.

She took several deep breaths. David wouldn't leave her for good. He loved her. People who loved each other did not leave permanently. When he was ready to tell her the cause of his outburst, they would work it out together. Together they could conquer anything.

She sat at her dinette table until one o'clock in the morning. Then she managed to drag herself into the bedroom and collapse onto the bed. He'd call. He had to.

He didn't. Not the next day, nor the next, nor the next. But Kathlyn waited. She cleaned and baked until her freezer was full. She missed Mass on Sunday for the first time since she'd had the chicken pox at seven. At least ten times each day she checked to make sure her phone was still working.

On Monday morning she called him at work. He had left on an extended trip, and his secretary had no idea where he was or when he'd return. Reality set in, and with it the devastation she had so carefully been warding off.

She sat on her couch, a pillow hugged tightly to her, and tried to think. She couldn't begin to imagine what had set David off. He had accused her of trying to control his life, but he had to know that wasn't true. Something else had scared him. But what?

She examined their entire relationship. Since leaving the convent, she'd known that one day she'd marry. She'd met David and had fallen in love. Her faith, her belief that God would provide, had made the whole thing so simple for her. Was there such a thing as too much faith? Had she been wrong all these years, relying on God's providence? No! She would not question her faith, too.

"Please, God. I'm so lost. What is it you want me to do?"

She didn't want to see anyone and didn't want anyone to see her. She stayed in her apartment for another week, leaving only to attend Mass—at a different church, so she wouldn't have to face Father Flynn. Dressed in her caftan, she wandered aimlessly around the apartment. As often as she could, she slept to forget. The meals she cooked went mostly uneaten.

Damn you, David St. John. No! "Oh, please, dear God, I didn't mean it." Where was he? Was he all right? Was he working himself into exhaustion? Why didn't he call?

On the next Wednesday, exactly two weeks after David had left, she went down to her mailbox and was shocked back into the world. Her last paycheck was crammed in an overflowing bundle of junk mail and bills. Life, with its many obligations, went on whether she wanted it to or not.

She opened her checkbook and noticed the last two checks she had written—one for her nonreturnable bridal gown and one for David's ring. She looked down at her finger and twisted the band of diamonds and sapphires. She remembered how David had lovingly placed it on her finger and sealed his pledge with a kiss. The jewels shimmered amid the sunlight and her tears as she slowly removed the ring.

She wrote out the checks for the bills at hand. She wrote another for next month's rent and one for her car payment. She figured she could live where she was for two more months. Then her savings would be completely depleted.

She took a deep breath and got on with the business of starting over, of survival. She called the school board office. All the music positions had been filled. With budgets the way they were, no school could afford to hire an extra teacher. She knew that the woman taking her place in the string quartet needed the extra money, so she would not beg Phil to take her back. She called the symphony orchestra's office and learned that the cello section was not only filled but had a waiting list.

She retrieved the Sunday paper from the stack of unread ones and opened it to the classified ads. Waitress. She wasn't afraid of the hard work involved, but figured she'd need two such jobs to make ends meet. She couldn't drive an eighteen-wheeler. She could sing, though! If she moved to a cheaper apartment and performed well enough to bring in some tips, singing in a nightclub would do. She called the number in the ad and was told to come by that afternoon for an audition.

It took her an hour and a half to camouflage the ravages the past weeks had taken on her looks. She dressed in an outfit she had outgrown the year before, one that wasn't too nun-ish. She gathered up a stack of pop music sheets and headed out the door.

The club was first class, the manager a member of her church. After settling on a comfortable musical key, she and the band began to sing and play in sync. The band improvised, and Kathlyn flowed right along with them. They hired her to begin the following night. They would perform Thursday through Sunday nights, and on Tuesdays and Wednesdays she would play and sing at the piano bar. With the addition of Tuesday's and Wednesday's salary, she wouldn't have to move to another apartment.

On the way home she stopped at a secondhand store and bought three black, formal gowns.

Thursday morning she practiced with the band. That night, as nervous as she'd ever been, Kathlyn Marie McDaniel made her singing debut with the Atlanta Hot Stuff. On Saturday night the place was packed. Word of mouth had drawn in the SRO crowd. By the next Saturday the owner was taking reservations only and had raised the cover charge. Kathlyn and the band got a raise.

On Tuesdays and Wednesdays she dressed less formally. Since she was continuing to lose weight—without David, she had little appetite—she had to take in most of her clothes. She played at a piano bar, suiting her music to the crowd. On the first Tuesday, she was hit with a group of men on convention. She played request after request, often having the men join in with her. She turned down four requests for an after-hours performance, but the men took it well and continued to fill the tip bowl. On Wednesday Kathlyn wasn't sure she'd make it through the night. The club was filled with lovers, asking for love songs and sentimental ballads.

A month after David's departure, Father Flynn cornered her on the street and invited her to the rectory for brunch. Kathlyn could do nothing but face the inevitable.

"He did it to you, didn't he, girl?"

"If you mean that he left me, the answer is yes." Kathlyn tried to be brave. She had sworn she wouldn't cry over him anymore. The tears flowed, anyway. "I still can't understand it. I don't know what I did wrong, or even if it was me." She filled Father in on David's parting shots.

"Listen, honey," the priest said, his big hand covering hers in an offer of comfort, "you didn't do anything. He wasn't sure in his own mind. I'd like to tell you he'll come back once he works it out, but I don't want to give you false hope."

Kathlyn wiped her eyes and staunchly faced the future. "I appreciate that, and I know I can't pin my hopes on a might-be. I think he's gone for good. He told me a long time ago that he wasn't interested in marriage, that he'd make a lousy husband. I didn't believe him. I still don't, but I can't change his mind for him."

She left the rectory two hours later and went into the church. She sat in a cushioned pew directly in the kaleidoscopic colors of the sun's rays shining through a stained-glass window.

In the quiet of the church, where the smell of the

recently extinguished candles filled her senses, and the sanctuary light burned in its red holder to remind her of the Lord's presence, Kathlyn took a look at her life. Without David. She still loved him, but that would have to pass. She had to get him out of her heart, so that she could love the man who would become her husband. She looked at the modern statue of Mary and Joseph with Jesus as a young boy. The marble faces transformed themselves in Kathlyn's watery eyes. Mary smiled, the young Jesus grinned, and Joseph, with a parenthesis grin, beamed at both of them.

"Ah, this is the life," David said as he flopped back on the grass and lowered his Fenner's Garage cap over his eyes. He'd lie here in the sun and let the damned bobber on his line bob all it wanted to. He didn't feel like cleaning fish. From now on he was only going to do whatever he felt like doing.

And women? Well, they could just go sink their claws into some other game. Damn, he couldn't go anywhere without them bugging him.

After that scene with the ex-nun who would remain nameless, he'd stormed back to his office and then immediately flown to Alaska.

Even that hadn't been far enough. The waitress in the bar he had attended regularly had come right out and asked him for a quickie in the back room. When he'd spent a few days in a small Alaskan village no one had ever heard of, he'd encountered yet another starving female. Not that he could really blame that one. The village was extremely remote, and there hadn't been much in the way of male companionship up there.

Now, after flying aimlessly from one city to the next, he had come home to his grandfather's to roost. That's exactly what he'd do—roost. He'd invent something, if he felt like it. He'd travel for short periods of time, when he felt like it. He'd fish or tinker with projects.

Just as soon as he felt like it.

He sat up when the fishing pole was yanked from his hands. "Stupid fish," he muttered as he pulled in the big perch. "Don't you know better than to be suckered in by a bare hook?" He unhooked the fish and sent it splashing back into the pond. "Probably a male." He lay back down and reached into his pocket for a cigarette. Males were always being suckered into something.

David felt the sharp jab in his side and sat up, shouting at his grandfather. "What the hell did you kick me for, old man? That hurt."

"Couldn't have hurt that much considering the spare tire you're sporting around your middle."

"I haven't got a spare tire, and you know it. I'm still in top shape."

"Yeah, and I'm the queen of England. When are you going to shave?"

"When I feel like it." David grumbled and got to his feet. Another stupid fish had gotten caught. He pulled it in and took it off the hook. He stared at it for a moment and then threw it back into the water.

"Not much sense fishing if you're not going to keep them."

"It's relaxing. Or it was when I was alone."

"Well, if you want to be alone, you'll have to move somewhere else. Why don't you go back to your apartment in Atlanta and check on your businesses?"

"Because . . ."

"I know. Don't tell me. You don't feel like it. Come on, let's go to the house. It's lunchtime."

Kevin served up soup and sandwiches and waited until they had finished the meal before saying anything else. He poured them each a cup of strong, black coffee and sat down across from his grandson.

"All right, David. What's troubling you?"

"Nothing." David answered automatically, but then looked at the raised gray eyebrow. "All right. If you have to know, I'm thinking of retiring."

"Retiring? You're only thirty!"

"Yeah, I turned thirty last week. That's when I decided. I've made enough money. I've worked hard for ten years now and don't feel like doing it anymore. There's more to life than working, you know."

"For most people, maybe, but work is a big part of your life. It's what you enjoy doing most. You mean to tell me that you're going to lie around, get fatter, and guzzle beer all day? And, for Pete's sake, put out that damn cigarette. You're smelling up the place something awful."

David stubbed out his cigarette and wrapped his arms around his middle. Hell and damnation, he *was* getting a tire! He was getting fat, his eyes were sinking in from too much beer, his lungs were ready to explode from too many cigarettes. He was going to hell, and it was all *her* fault! No, he wouldn't think about her.

"Say," his grandfather asked, "whatever happened to that girl you mentioned a couple of months ago? Kathlyn, wasn't it? Kathlyn Marie McDaniel. Thought that had a nice musical sound to it."

Kathlyn! He hadn't uttered her name, had tried not to think her name in weeks, and now the old coot said it right out loud! "I don't want to talk about her. Now. Never. You hear me?"

"Well, hell, Mrs. Peters down the lane could hear you, boy. What'd this Kathlyn do to you?"

"Turned me into this, for one thing."

"Nonsense! No one can make you do anything you don't want to do."

"I mean it, Grandpap. She tricked me into loving her. Once I fell, she did everything she could to change me. Hell, I couldn't go for more than five minutes without thinking about her. She was always there influencing my business decisions. And damned if she didn't insist on turning me into a Catholic. She even called in a priest to help her do it. 'Take instructions', the priest said. You know how those Catholics are."

"Can't say as I do."

"Well, let me tell you. They're weird. She talks to statues and everything. Creepy."

"And when you wouldn't turn Catholic, she dumped you?"

"No. I dumped her. I finally put my foot down and told her I'd continue to take care of my own soul."

"Good for you, boy. Now, when are you going to do it?"

"Do what?"

"Start taking care of yourself. And if you say when you damn well feel like it, I'll throw you in that pond out there."

David's head lowered and his shoulders slumped. "I don't know, Grandpap, but I guess it'd better be soon."

Kevin rose and placed his hand comfortingly on David's shoulder before leaving the room. Something needed to be done. And quick!

"Ms. McDaniel, there's a visitor to see you," the apartment manager announced over the phone.

"Who is it, Millie?'"

"He says it's about David St. John."

Oh, dear God, something's happened to David! "Send him up, Millie."

Kathlyn flung open the door the minute she heard the knock. "Is he okay? What's happened?"

"Well, he ain't dead or sick or nothing, if that's what you mean."

Kathlyn gaped at the gruff old man and automatically stepped back as he walked into her apartment. It was either move or be pushed out of the way. He was David's grandfather, she was sure.

"Won't you come in, Mr. St. John?"

"You're kind of a mess, you know that. You been lying around doing nothing, too?"

Kathlyn had no idea what he was talking about, but bristled. She began undoing her hot rollers. "I'm in the process of getting ready for work. Please say what it is you want to see me about and then leave."

"Work? I thought you were a teacher."

"At your grandson's request, I took a year's leave of absence so we could enjoy our first year of marriage together. So far it's been a real delight."

"You mean he married you?"

"No, he only got as far as the starting gate." She walked over to the kitchen counter and picked up a wrapped package. "Here. You might as well give him back the ring. I had it ready to go in tomorrow's mail."

As Kevin reached for the package, he noticed the circles of fatigue under her eyes. Pretty eyes. Kind of intriguing looking at them under those sleepy eyelids. Her hand was shaking as she gave him the package, clasping the box for one moment before releasing it. Poor child.

No. He wouldn't soften toward her. She was destroying David's life.

"Kind of skinny, aren't you?"

Kathlyn's back stiffened and she looked the old man straight in the eyes. Eyes the same chocolate color as

David's. "I'll have you know that I'm a perfect size seven."

"Probably look better in a ten or twelve."

"Twelve?" Kathlyn gasped, and then couldn't help laughing. The man was so outrageous.

"Ain't nothing funny about what you did to David, girl. Nothing funny at all!"

"What I . . ." She saw that he'd meant what he'd said, saw his love and concern for his grandson. Her voice softened. "I don't know what David has told you, Mr. St. John, but I honestly did nothing to him—at least nothing that I'm aware of."

Kevin looked deeply into her eyes and saw that she spoke the truth. He also saw the pain that matched David's. "If you have time, could we sit and talk? I'd like to hear your side of what happened."

What *had* happened? A day hadn't gone by that Kathlyn hadn't tried to figure it out. Maybe in voicing her confusion and heartbreak, she could finally find release from the pain.

"I'll call the club and tell them I'll be a little late this evening."

"Club?"

"I perform at a nightclub. Tonight it's just me and the piano, so it should be all right."

She made the call and then fixed them each a cup of coffee. Sitting on the couch across from him, she related everything that had happened between her and David from the moment they'd met until the day he'd left.

"And did this priest of yours try to convert David?"

"Heavens, no. He only told David he needed to take a few instructions, so he'd understand some of the beliefs that would affect our lives.

"Now, I really must finish getting ready for work."

"Go ahead. I'll pour myself another cup of coffee and take you. No, don't argue. I want to see you perform. I'll drive you home again."

"If you're sure." Actually she was looking forward to spending more time with him. She liked him, not only because he was David's grandfather, but because he was a nice old bird.

"I'm sure. Now, scoot, or you're really going to be late." Kevin poured himself the coffee and sat again in the rocking chair. He believed her. There was something that didn't quite ring true about David's side of it. And now the poor girl was left to handle the rejection, not knowing what the real cause had been. Kevin had a pretty good idea what that cause was. He had come here ready to give this woman a good what for. Now he was ready to kick David a good hard one right in the behind for not talking to Kathlyn or to him.

David tossed and turned, unable to sleep. He'd known it was going to happen, had dreaded every night the moment when his mind overcame the restraint he had placed on it. He'd also known that tonight would be the night. Just with his grandfather's mentioning of her name, he knew the time had come. He rose from the bed and donned his sweat pants and shirt. He'd run. He'd begin getting himself back into shape while he tried to push off the inevitable for a while longer. He didn't want to think about Kathlyn, to remember the hurt look in her eyes and the tears on her face when he'd left her. Most of all, he didn't want to remember how sweet it had been with her.

He quietly went out to the porch and did his warm-up exercises. He was breathing heavily by the time he finished them. He took off, jogging at a leisurely pace, and had to stop halfway down the long driveway to catch his breath. How many damn cigarettes had he smoked in the past weeks? Enough, it seemed, to clog his lungs but good. And all that beer and lying around hadn't helped, either. He took off again, more slowly this time. With excruciating effort, he made it to the end of the driveway.

He'd just decided to walk back when his grandfather's car rounded the corner. David straightened his shoulders and jogged until the car was out of sight. He stopped and put his hands on his knees, gasping for breath. Without warning, tears spouted from his eyes, and his shoulders began to shake with wracking sobs. He sank to the ground and buried his face in his hands.

God, he missed her—everything about her. He felt empty. He *was* empty. "Kathlyn!" he cried into the night. "Kathlyn, damn it, I need you!"

The tears flowed harder, and thoughts tumbled one right on top of the other. She had loved him in a way he would never find again. He had accused her of taking over his being. What nonsense. She was the kind of lifeline a person could only know when truly loved.

He rose from the asphalt and began a slow trot back toward the house, letting the wind dry his tears. He still didn't have all the answers, but this time he was determined to get them.

Just as David had hoped, his grandfather was waiting for him. David dropped down on the porch swing next to the old man and tried to catch his breath.

After some minutes, Kevin quietly broke the silence. "I went to see your Kathlyn."

"How does she look? What's she doing? Is she okay?"

Kevin turned toward his grandson. "She's doing fine. Looks a little thin and hollow-eyed, but she's okay. You love her, don't you?"

David closed his eyes. "With everything in me."

"Then why the hell aren't you going to marry her?"

David jumped to his feet. "Don't you think I want to? Do you have any idea what I'd give to spend the rest of my life with her?"

He folded his arms across his chest, his hands clenched into fists. "How the hell long would it be before we felt the trap? Would I go the way Mom did, because I tried to curb my abilities? Or, if I couldn't, would I kill Kathlyn's love through neglect?"

"Spit and hellfire! David, your parents' stupidity is not hereditary. They caused their own problems unnecessarily. I thought you knew what went on."

David sat down again, afraid to get his hopes up, afraid not to. "Tell me."

"John was about twenty-two when he met your mother. He'd gone to work as a junior partner in her father's bank. Sarah came home that summer, and the two of them fell head over heels in love. She had just graduated with top honors in genetic engineering. Your dad was from common stock. You know your grandma and I weren't long on education. That bothered your dad. He was afraid that Sarah would go out and meet someone else, someone smarter than he. So he kept her chained to the house. John got her to promise him that she wouldn't work until after you were in school.

"According to your ma, that was exactly what she wanted. She was tired of being poked and prodded because of her intellect. She wanted to lead an ordinary life.

"To give your dad the benefit of the doubt, I don't think he knew just how gifted Sarah was. I think he'd have encouraged her to do all the good she could have done, if only he'd known.

"Anyway, after Sarah's father died, John became

president of the bank. He used his position as another way to keep Sarah from going out into the work force. He asked her to help him with the social end of the business.

"Sarah knew how important it was to your dad that she stay close to him, and she thought it was because he loved her so much, he wanted to keep her near.

"She tried, David, but her mind couldn't stop working. On the sly she worked on those puzzles and games you and she played. It was an outlet and a means of helping the world, if only in a small way.

"Eventually, it wasn't enough. More and more often John'd come home and find Sarah bent over books or lost in thought over something or another while supper was burning on the stove. His fear of losing her increased, and he tried to tie her closer to him, to the house, to you.

"One day he came home, worried sick because she hadn't answered the phone. He found her staring off into space, mumbling incoherently.

"He never forgave himself. He'd supported and encouraged everything in you, son, but he'd killed those same abilities in his wife.

"I can see why he told you marriage was a trap. Both of your parents were caught in it. John was the one who sprang it. Sarah never asked to be set free."

"What a god-awful waste!" David exclaimed. Everything Grandpap had said confirmed what David had suspected. What miracles his mother could have performed. What lifesaving miracles she could have come up with.

Nothing David did could prevent what had already happened, but he wasn't going to ruin two other lives.

"Thanks, Grandpap." David rose tiredly.

"You going to go see Kathlyn?"

David swung on the old man. "See her? Good God, no! I can't let history repeat itself."

"Fool!" Kevin shouted. "I didn't tell you all that so you'd give up on life. I told you so you wouldn't make the same mistake."

"Exactly. I'm not getting married. Ever!"

When David's temper was up, Kevin could usually get him to come out with his hidden feelings. "Does Kathlyn know about your abilities?"

"Yeah. So?"

"Has she ever seen you go into one of those intellectual trances when you're working out a problem?"

"She's seen me weird out." It happened on one of the last days he'd stayed at her apartment.

"What'd she do while you were off in genius land?"

"I don't know. Played the cello." He vaguely remembered hearing it in the background while he'd sat in her sun-room. "Did laundry." When he'd come out of the study, she'd been folding wash at her dining table. They'd sat at the table littered with folded and unfolded clothes and talked for an hour about his idea. Mostly he'd talked, and she had listened and encouraged and even thrown in a few suggestions.

"She made me lunch." David relaxed with a smile and then sat back down on the swing, making it jump and then glide. "I remember knocking over the plate containing bread crusts while gesturing with my hands. She'd made me a sandwich, and I must have eaten it. I'll have to tell her that I don't like crusts."

"Yes, son, you tell her. A wife needs to know such things about her husband."

"We're not like Mom and Dad, are we?"

Kevin could hear the relief and pure, sweet joy in David's voice. "No, but you have to talk to her about the important things. That was your ma and pa's fatal mistake. Lack of communication was their downfall.

"She has a right, David, to know about your parents. About your fears, your hopes and plans. You've kept her in the dark for too long. Remember, marriage is a two-way support team. I saw that girl. She's just special enough to be the one for you."

David frowned. It had just dawned on him that he'd tried to squelch Kathlyn's career. Those kids she taught needed her, and he'd selfishly asked her to give it up in order to keep him and his ego secure. What a damn fool he'd been.

Both men rose from the porch swing. Kevin's bones creaked and his muscles ached, but his heart was rejoicing. David and Kathlyn belonged together, just like he and his Maggie had.

"Grandpap?" David stopped with one hand on the screen door handle. "You always claim you're common stock. How did you make your fortune?"

"From common stock, boy. Your grandma and I liked to fiddle around with the market."

David chuckled. "Good night. And thanks."

"You're welcome, son. Good luck."

"Luck? I think a few prayers will go further."

"I think you're right."

At five the next morning David was out jogging again. When he returned to the kitchen, he saw the package from Kathlyn. He unwrapped the box, opened it, and stared at the ring. Then he snapped the box shut.

Coffee was in order, and then some breakfast. He sipped the brew, longing for a cigarette to go with it. Instead of giving in, he took the remaining packs from the carton and threw them into the trash. He'd give up those nasty things again, but no way was he going to give up Kathlyn. No matter how long it took him, he was going to convince her that they belonged together. And this time he was going to let her see the entire man.

He went to work, surprising his staff after his long absence. He instructed his secretary to make an appointment with Father Flynn. After only an hour or so, he discovered that the office had run exceptionally well without him. He spent another hour going meticulously over everything that had been done and the companies still under his umbrella. Six. He had only six companies, all worth saving. He called a meeting of the staff.

"Okay, ladies and gentleman, we're down to the final tally. I don't think this is going to come as too much of a shock, but I want out of the whole thing. I have six companies left, and am going to offer them to you first. The price will be minimal, a compensation for disbanding the company. I thought that the way you all take to organizing and managing, you might want to head up your own companies."

Three of the eight people opted to retire instead of taking on a company. The other five bought the ones they were most interested in running.

"That only leaves the turkey farm, but I guess I can handle one."

"I'd like to make an offer on the farm," his secretary said quietly. "My husband has to ease up a bit on work, and I think a turkey farm in California might just fit the bill."

"Well, that takes care of that." David grinned. He felt marvelously free. "I sincerely want to thank each and every one of you for your years of dedication. We did one hell of a job."

Amid a chorus of agreement and best wishes, the group disbanded, anxious to begin their new careers.

David sat back for a moment and gloried in his success. It felt damn good to go out a winner. Into what? Teaching. He had shrugged off the idea at one time, but the excitement and ideas about what he'd do had continued to grow and expand. However, first things first.

He went to his local gym and pumped some iron, stopped and had his hair cut, and then headed back to the office. At six o'clock he showed up at the rectory. Father Flynn answered the door and offered David a handshake.

"So, my boy, you finally got your head on straight."

"Takes some a little longer than others. Pray it's not too late."

"I don't think so. I think she's still very much in love with you. What happened, anyway?"

At two o'clock that same afternoon, Kathlyn walked into Tara Haven Nursing Home. She shifted the potted plant in her hand. Then, wondering if she was doing the right thing, she slowed her step. After Kevin's visit the night before, Kathlyn had remembered the conversation with David about his mother being in a nursing home. Kathlyn was tired of the ups and downs she had been going through since David had left. One minute she'd be filled with despair, knowing that their relationship was over; the next she'd remember how perfect they were together, about all the plans and dreams she had had for their life together.

But enough was enough! Kevin hadn't exactly encouraged her to continue hoping for David's return, but he hadn't discouraged her, either. After hours of calling one nursing home after the other, Kathlyn had found the one in which David's mother, Sarah, was staying. Perhaps she could shed some light on why David would not marry and help free her from this limbo. Taking a deep, steadying breath, Kathlyn punched the elevator button.

"Mrs. St. John?" Kathlyn asked softly, entering the room. Sarah was dozing in a comfortable rocking chair, knitting needles resting on her stomach. The white blouse and gray slacks looked neat but were loose-fitting on Sarah's small frame. Her salt-and-pepper hair was brushed and flowed down past her shoulders.

"Yes?" Sleepy eyelids lifted to reveal soft doe's eyes.

Kathlyn came all the way into the room and sat on the hassock at the lady's feet. "I'm Kathlyn McDaniel, a . . . friend of David's."

The brown eyes sharpened, seemed to laser into Kathlyn. "Friend?" The one word was filled with derision.

Taken aback at Sarah's sharp tone, Kathlyn stumbled over her reply. "Yes, ma'am."

Sarah's intent gaze lingered and probed. "No," she finally said, steel in her voice. "You are more than a friend, or at least you hope to be. But let me tell you, young lady," she said, raising the knitting needles and shaking them under Kathlyn's nose, "nobody is going to marry David, so you can go and set your little trap for someone else."

"But, Mrs. St. John . . ." Kathlyn stammered, afraid of the flashing eyes and flying needles. She stood and moved away.

Sarah rose to pace the room, finally stopping directly in front of Kathlyn.

"What do you have to offer him? Have you a mind fit to keep up with David's? Have you the patience to wait while he spends days working out solutions to problems most people wouldn't even consider questioning? You don't look capable of supporting his intellectual pursuits, much less putting up with him when he ignores you.

"Don't even think it. Don't you dare ruin my son by trapping him in marriage like John trapped me. He can beg all he wants to, but I won't go back to him. I will not cater to any man again. Let him find his pleasure with other women, I don't care. I must work!"

A nurse rushed into the room. "What's going on in here? Oh, darling, you're upset. Come, rest for a while."

"Rest? There is no way I can rest. I wasted too many years away from my work. I have to catch up, do what has to be done." Sarah snatched the potted plant from Kathlyn's hands and tore off a leaf. She took it to her worktable and inserted it under the microscope.

Look, Darla," she addressed the nurse. "Look at the rare plant the university sent over for me to work with."

"I'll be there in just a minute, Sarah. You begin and I'll catch up." The nurse motioned to Kathlyn and then escorted her out of the room.

"I'm sorry, miss, but I can't have you disturbing Sarah. She's fine most of the time, but one never knows what will set her off. The poor dear's had a rough time of it."

Kathlyn was in shock. She tried to smile at the nurse and apologize, but her words came out stammering and pathetic.

She walked to the elevator and punched the down button, her mind whirling. When she exited the elevator she saw the sign indicating the chapel. She entered the serene atmosphere of the green-carpeted, rich oak-paneled room and seated herself in the front pew.

Kathlyn knew that David sometimes went off into mental forays, but God had given him his talents. She would never begrudge him that, or demand he curb them in order to cater to her. She'd feed him, take care of him, and make sure he had the working environment he needed. She and their children would understand when he went into his creating mode.

Even with her support, though, would David feel as if he had wasted, as Sarah evidently had, a good bit of his life by marrying? No. That just didn't make sense. She had felt a longing in David, a desire for something more, but hadn't known what else a person of his capabilities and rich life could need. Until now.

He needed her! Not some other woman. What did that woman upstairs know? Kathlyn knew she was exactly what David needed to make him whole.

If only he had talked to her, told her his fears, they could have straightened this out weeks ago. Well, she was going to confront him, and he was going to talk! Not in brief, vague answers, but with total communication. If he still wanted her out of his life, she was going to know exactly why!

David stood before the mirror in his bedroom, buttoning his blue suit coat. It still fit. He ran his hands over the slight roundness at his waist and shook his head ruefully. That crazy old man had had him believing he'd gone to pot. Well, David admitted, he had been on his way.

He entered the Razzle Dazzle Club ten minutes before closing, his hands wet, the ring box burning a hole in his breast pocket.

David looked up at the spotlighted stage in the dimly

lit, smoke-filled room. The music soared, and the audience clapped in rhythm. David was stunned at his first glimpse of Kathlyn in over two months. Her impact was even more powerful than the first night he had met her. She moved around the stage dressed in a strapless black velvet dress, giving the audience teasing glimpses of one shapely leg as a side split parted with her movements. He wanted, with an urge so strong he hoped he could restrain himself, to run up onstage, kiss her, scoop her up into his arms, and take her to her dressing room. Instead he sat down and watched her play up to her audience. She was singing a wicked little number called "You Got What It Takes." He laughed with the rest of the audience when she rubbed the head of a bald man, and whistled when she swung her sassy hips to the sexy little beat.

During the clapping and cheering, she smiled and slid a stool to stage front. The band modulated into another number. The audience grew silent at the opening bars of a slow ballad. The hair on the back of David's neck rose when he recognized the melody of "The Wind Beneath My Wings." The husky sound of Kathlyn's voice singing one of the songs that reminded him of her sensitized every nerve ending in his body. The spotlight turned her teardrops to crystals. Her image shimmered through the moisture in his own eyes.

"Oh, angel," he whispered. Well, if she was going to have wings, so was he! She'd just better help him earn them.

The lights went out immediately after the final notes. The haunting melody hung suspended in the silent room. Applause suddenly burst forth and the glaring lights flicked back on.

Kathlyn was wiping her eyes. That song made her

cry every time. She stood and smiled at the audience, took her bows with the band, and left the stage.

As she was removing her makeup, a knock sounded on her dressing room door. She had already changed into loose-fitting jeans and a Falcon High sweat shirt. "Come in."

Gary, the leader of the band, entered. "Hey, love."

"Hey, yourself." Gary was a good old boy and one heck of a fine musician.

"Got some good news and bad news. The band has been asked to go on tour with an up-and-coming vocalist. I'm sorry, I know this leaves you in a bind."

"Nonsense." What was one more starting over? "You deserve it. Congratulations."

"Thanks. Murrey said you could continue to sing on Tuesdays and Wednesdays, but the replacement band already has a vocalist. It won't be much money, though. I wish I could help."

"Don't worry about me. I'll find something. I've been saving everything I could from this job, so I'm not destitute."

"You sure, love?"

"I'm sure. I'll be watching the charts for your name, and I'll buy every one of your records, so go out there and make me proud."

"Will do." He leaned down and kissed her on the cheek. "You know you could make it in the business if you wanted to. You have one hell of a fine voice."

"Thanks, Gary, but I don't think this is the career I want. It's been great knowing and working with you."

"Same here."

The first thing Kathlyn was going to do was confront David. But not tonight. It was late, and she was simply too weary. It was a relief to be through with this job.

The hours and energy spent on the stage were grueling. She'd find something. What choice did she have?

Gary reentered the room and placed a cassette recorder and tape on the table in front of her. "Some guy asked me to give this to you. Take care, okay?"

"Okay," Kathlyn replied absently. The note on the tape had her heart beating too fast and her hands shaking. It was in David's handwriting. PLAY ME. PLEASE!

"Please." Startled, Kathlyn looked up into the dusty, chipped mirror and saw his reflection. Under the glaring bare bulb of the ceiling light, he looked good—tired, nervous, but handsome in the blue suit that was her favorite. Her eyes met his and saw the plea in them. She picked up the tape and clumsily inserted it into the player.

Johnny Mathis' voice filled the room as he sang "The Twelfth of Never." Tracked over the song, David's voice filled her heart.

"I've told you that I love you, and I meant it. It's the needing that scared me. I need you more than even this song proclaims, but it's all right. Needing, I've learned, is as much a part of loving as desire. Will you marry me, Kathlyn Marie? I love you now, and will continue to love you until the twelfth of never, and beyond."

Kathlyn's eyes were moist, her throat blocked. She slowly turned and looked at him. "It can't be like before, David. You can't shut me out."

"I've learned that the hard way, love. I hadn't meant to do that. I always thought I would be alone, that I could only count on myself to solve my problems. You'll have to remind me, even bully me, but I want to share everything. I'm so lonely, angel. Please let me share my life with you."

Kathlyn was up from the bench and into his waiting

arms a second after his final words. Tears poured from her eyes as she hugged him.

"Tighter, angel. Hold me tighter."

Kathlyn squeezed as hard as she could and then lifted her tear-soaked face. The kiss was achingly gentle, lovingly sweet. It was the fulfillment of the rainbow's promises.

"I love you, David."

"Kathlyn, I've always loved you, but I was afraid of how much I needed you. Afraid I'd turn out like . . ."

"Like your mother," she finished softly.

David's eyes widened in surprise.

Kathlyn rested her hand tenderly on his cheek. "I went to see her."

David sighed. "Then you know. I promise never to keep anything from you again." His lips descended to meet hers and seal his vow.

They kissed and held on to each other as the final strains of the song drifted into the air around them. They looked at each other through moist eyes and smiles. And then the realization hit them that the long heartbreak was over. They grinned and hugged again and then laughed in joyous harmony.

David's hands roamed hungrily over her body. "You've lost weight, sweetheart."

Kathlyn found his love handles. "And you've gained some."

David shrugged. "I didn't feel like doing anything without you to share it."

"And I had to stay busy to keep sane."

"I'm sorry, Kathlyn. So very, very—"

She placed a gentle finger on his lips. "Shh, darling. It's over."

Unable to look away from her, he nibbled on her

finger. "You want to get married a week from Saturday? Michael says we can."

"You mean you talked to Father Flynn?"

"Yeah. Kind of a weird guy for a priest. Nice, though. So, what do you say? A week from Saturday okay with you?"

His body was as stiff as a board. He seemed to be holding his breath.

"Yes, as it happens, I'm free then."

"Good." David tried to act matter-of-fact, but every muscle in his body seemed to release tension at once. He lowered his head and rested it alongside of her neck, breathing in her familiar wildflower scent. "After we're married, angel, you must know you can teach or do *anything* you want that will make you happy. You don't have to go traipsing around with me."

Kathlyn raised her eyes in a heartfelt thank-you. She once more ran her fingers through the silky curls at the nape of David's neck and felt the strands wrap welcomingly around her fingers. "Since I have until next fall before another term starts, I think I'll tag along and watch my genius at work."

David lifted his head and grimaced. "Some genius. I couldn't even recognize my own salvation until I'd almost lost you."

"Why don't we go home?"

"I am home," he said. "As long as you're with me."

EPILOGUE

"Beth, Mary, phone!"

The two teenage girls came bounding around the corner, blond ponytails flying. "Thanks, Dad."

David went into the remodeled kitchen of the old ranch house shaking his head, a frown drawing his eyebrows together. "I don't like it, Kathlyn."

Kathlyn knew what was coming. David loved his twin daughters. He had never missed a piano or dance recital, had coached Little League and kissed hurts away. He had agonized over every stage of their childhoods. She knew this next phase of their lives was going to be the hardest on him.

"Elizabeth and Mary are too young to be having boys sniffing around, constantly calling. Going out."

Kathlyn poured David a cup of coffee and handed it to him. "They're fourteen, starting high school in the fall. It's time, love."

David seated himself at the oak kitchen table and groaned. "I'm not ready."

"I know." She kissed his cheek. "But you've made it through every other level of their development. You'll make it through this one. They're good girls."

David sighed. Both girls looked so much like their mother, and they had her trust in human nature. For Pete's sake, Kathlyn had gone out with him, and all he'd wanted was to get her into bed! Kathlyn was wrong. He wasn't going to make it through this stage!

Beth entered the room, glowing and exuberant. "Can Mary and I go to the movies tonight?"

"What time? With whom?"

"The nine-o'clock show. Jim and Scott."

David's reply was firm. "The seven-o'clock show, and find some others to go with you."

"M-o-o-om!"

"B-e-e-eth!" Kathlyn returned.

"Mary," the girl yelled on her way out of the room, "see if Sam and Dinah and Carrie and Slick can go. Dad says . . ." Her voice trailed off.

Slick? Oh, God!

"What's going on?" twelve-year-old Michael asked while heading for the refrigerator and the milk carton.

"Nothing," David answered. "And use a glass."

The two exchanged grins. Michael already had the exciting good looks of his father. He also topped David in IQ. Both questioned, figured, and probed "what ifs." Father and son had joint patents on four successful inventions, and Michael was getting college credit for attending one of the classes David taught.

In two years her baby would be heading off to college. Alone, having to conquer the demons David had once had to face. But, with God's help, David's guidance, and her love and support, she knew Michael would be fine.

"The twins and I are going to Kevin's for an hour or so. Okay?" The boy was already on his way out of the room.

"Okay," both parents said simultaneously.

David coughed to cover his eagerness.

Kathlyn turned her back to hide the blush she felt heating her cheeks. She heard David's footsteps right before his arms slipped around her.

"A whole hour," he whispered into her ear.

Kathlyn turned and, putting her arms around his neck, fitted her body to his. She grinned teasingly, and David knew what was coming. He'd heard it often enough in their sixteen years of marriage. "But, David, we just did it last night. What with the passion calming down after the first year and all, I don't think . . ." He kissed her to shut her up and then hugged her. Tightly. "I had no idea, angel, none whatsoever, that love and passion could grow and deepen as ours have."

He swallowed hard and for a moment was overwhelmed by the intensity of that passion, by the love they shared. She was his life, his support, and, as he'd once suspected, his salvation. What had he ever done to deserve her? He raised his eyes heavenward. *Thanks!*

Her breath tickled his neck. Goose bumps rose on his flesh. Damn, but she was still the sexiest woman he'd ever seen.

"Upstairs or down?"

"Mmm," she pondered while relishing the wonderful aromas of his lime after-shave and freshly showered skin.

Their night loving was always spectacular. Sometimes slow and easy, sometimes fast and furious, sometimes a combination of all four. But there was another kind of thrill—racy, deliciously wicked, daring—in snatching an afternoon delight. Her heart beat faster as scenes from past stolen moments ran through her head.

"Upstairs," she decided. She wiggled against him and lifted her head to watch his eyes deepen to dark chocolate. Lord, the man was handsome, yet he was so much more. He was a man to depend on, to laugh with, a man who shared with her every private wish, her God-sent grand passion.

She fluttered her eyelashes and then winked seductively. She moved her hands over his shoulders, slowly under his arms, tantalizingly across his back, and then down to his tight jeans-encased buttocks. The familiar quickening of her body made her breath shallow. Every time she aroused David, she found herself getting doubly so.

"Yes. Definitely upstairs," she whispered naughtily, tightening her hands on his bottom, rubbing herself against his arousal.

David groaned and clasped her shorts-clad posterior to anchor them together.

She still had a body to slay dragons for, and the seductive moves to make a man determined to do so forever. In their bedroom, she stripped teasingly, watching David's hungry expression. She came to him on the king-size bed laughing, flushed, naked, and aroused.

Nearly out of his mind with wanting her, he flipped her over and under him, entering her with one long, smooth stroke.

Lord, after sixteen years he thought he'd be used to the sensations of joining with his wife. After all this time, each time was still special. Loving his Kathlyn just got better and better.

"I love you, angel," he shouted in climax.

She joined him, whispering his name in awe and wonder. It was a sound he'd heard before. A sound he craved to hear again and again, all the way through eternity.

SHARE THE FUN . . .
SHARE YOUR NEW-FOUND TREASURE!!

You don't want to let your new books out of your sight? That's okay. Your friends can get their own. Order below.

No. 58 SWEET SEDUCTION by Allie Jordan
Libby wages war on Will—she'll win his love yet!

No. 59 13 DAYS OF LUCK by Lacey Dancer
Author Pippa Weldon finds her real-life hero in Joshua Luck.

No. 60 SARA'S ANGEL by Sharon Sala
Sara *must* get to Hawk. He's the only one who can help.

No. 61 HOME FIELD ADVANTAGE by Janice Bartlett
Marian shows John there is more to life than just professional sports.

No. 62 FOR SERVICES RENDERED by Ann Patrick
Nick's life is in perfect order until he meets Claire!

No. 63 WHERE THERE'S A WILL by Leanne Banks
Chelsea goes toe-to-toe with her new, unhappy business partner.

No. 64 YESTERDAY'S FANTASY by Pamela Macaluso
Melissa always had a crush on Morgan. Maybe dreams do come true!

No. 65 TO CATCH A LORELEI by Phyllis Houseman
Lorelei sets a trap for Daniel but gets caught in it herself.
